Somewhere

in

India

Chronicles of a Thriving Culture

By

Kirti Vyas

Cover Design: Poonam Hassija

Cover design by Poonam Hassija

This book is a work of fiction in as much as most of the events did not transpire in the order presented in any story. So, while all the anecdotes and vignettes in this book are derived from true incidents experienced by the author or her family members, each story is a patchwork quilt of two or three different episodes.

Also, even though many of the characters' names are based on the author's family or family's staff, the stories associated with their names may or may not have been experienced by them.

Dedicated to the love of my life

and my husband

Dhiresh,

who held me afloat while I coped

with the loss of my parents

Dhiraj and Bharti Sanghavi,

(1935 – 2024),

and helped me put one foot in front

of the other even when

I couldn’t see any path forward.

Contents

Section I

"India is not for beginners”

(A popular sentiment)

Introduction

The best love affair is usually the one we didn't have. It exists only in our minds, unmarred by the messiness of life. More often than not, it's a romance not even remotely based in reality.

That perfectly describes my relationship with India.

India was the stalwart lover I had spurned without a thought, even though it had sustained and steadied me from birth to thirty. And why did I do it? I abandoned all that was dearly familiar and traditionally sound because I had been wooed by western ways and because I was too young to know better. I'd fallen headlong into infatuation, captivated by the idea of unbridled freedom, and so I traveled tens of thousands of miles eagerly for such a life. Lured by a promise of plenty, I had inadvertently fled to a land where I was expected to shun the way I spoke, thought, and dressed. This new world sought to devalue my accomplishments, deride me often for being different, even demand that I change my accent. It rebuffed me in too many ways to count, but I stayed for the same reasons many people do in humiliating situations – because to leave was to admit to a lack of judgement.

Held back by slivers of shame and scads of stubbornness, I dug in, determined to restore my self-esteem on my own terms, if not carve my niche and to prove that I could make it against all odds. And I did. However, now that I am older, I have realized the foolishness of giving up years and years to justify any decision to anyone. Life is too short to waste time or to feel embarrassment over poor choices.

Age and reason have also taught me that had I stayed back and lived all my life in India, the truth would be vastly different from any illusions I've painted in my imagination. Like any lover or land, India is not perfect. The merciless for-profit media and the many compassionate storytellers have already covered that. Sensational news cater to the demand of an audience's innate negativity bias, which has been further honed by constant news feeds to seek, sympathize, and spread more sad and horrific news than what is good and wholesome in any society. In addition, since India is such an onslaught on the senses, many, especially tourists, may miss the underlying beauty of its caring communities and its enduring customs.

It's possible that even though the country presents the whole gamut of the truly noble and the purely evil, some visitors may be unlucky and come face-to-face with just its ugliest side. Afterall, the good and bad in any place is directly proportional to the number of humans it holds, and India being the most populated country in the world owns scores of every kind on the scale and then some. Lastly, the overwhelming sights, sounds, smells, and the sheer number of people may make it hard for even a seasoned traveler to learn about the fine fabric that binds its people. That thread of thought led to the weaving of the stories in this book. I wanted to share what I knew to be endearing and heartwarming about the land and people I love so much, and also because I believe that such stories need to be highlighted more in a world hurting for human connections.

In keeping with my goal of sharing and celebrating some of the things I love about India, I have included only anecdotes and stories in this collection that reveal an India untarnished by any adult anguish or ills of its society. These accounts may even appear to have been written through rose-tinted lenses – whether it's the advice given by life-weary but wise taxi drivers, comments of annoying but caring busybodies, or the back-bending service offered to most shoppers.

All in all, this book is a love letter to India. Like a love letter, it gushes over the strengths and beauty of one's beloved, finds the failings just amusing eccentricities, and even glosses over some of the most inherently offensive features. Everyone knows that love letters are never supposed to be a lineup of complaints, so if flaws are what you wish to find about India, you must look elsewhere. You will not find them in this book, except in the poem, "This is Home," which acknowledges its weaknesses without diminishing my sentiments.

As strongly as I feel about the matter, this collection would have not come together without the unwavering support of my family, especially my husband Dhiresh Vyas, my sister

Sejal Patel, and my niece-in-law and one of the daughters of my heart, Dr. Pooja Sancheti. I am so grateful to you all and also to the universe for including you in my world. Thank you to my sustaining sisterhood, which is not limited to Adele Josovitz, Aradhana Tyagi, Karen Kotchko, Komal Juneja, Leann Ratner, Mary Baker, Mona Jhaveri, and Sheila Patel among many others, who have supported me and helped me survive an exceptionally hard time.

I'm grateful to Dr. Pooja Sancheti and Victoria Sherrow for editing the stories and to Selin Ho and Amy Gershberg for reading the manuscript after all the changes were made for their keen insights that led to a few more meaningful improvements. Lastly, and extremely importantly, I'm thankful to Poonam Hassija for the fabulous cover illustration. It is easy to see that her work, too, is a labor of love.

With gratitude,
Kirti Vyas

1.

Somewhere in India

, we share, we care, and we mind other people's business

Background information / Vocabulary:

chakris - savory, crisp, pinwheel-shaped fried snacks made from rice flour, sesame seeds, and spices

chevdo - a crisp, savory mix that may include variations of fried or roasted cornflakes and or puffed rice, fried savory noodles, potato sticks, raisins, nuts, and spices to taste salty, sweet, tangy, and zesty in each mouthful.

Aayah - a girl or woman employed by a family to look after children, and help in other domestic tasks

Dadi-ma - Respected Grandmother

Bhaiya or Bhai - brother, sometimes a suffix after a proper name to address an older brother

Ji - a prefix or suffix to show respect, such as after a title, a name, or a sentence; “alright” or “yes”

Chole - a popular North Indian curry, made with chickpeas (also known as garbanzo beans) and several spices

dal - dried, split legumes, primarily lentils

Arrey-wah! - an expression that means “How wonderful!” (Note: Arrey-reh or Arrey is a sympathetic response to a mishap or bad news)

pedas - plural for “peda” and also referred to as “penda,” these are popular fudge-like, disc-shaped sweets made with milk solids, sugar, cardamom, nuts, and sometimes, saffron.

Swiggy - one of the several delivery services that bring food, medicines, among other things within minutes right to your door

Beta or Betu - beloved child

Chappal - a term for sandals, typically without a back strap

A CHILD’S HAND SNUCK IN through the circular design of the wrought-iron grill of an open window. Reaching a steel jar placed on the kitchen counter, the small fingers lifted the lid, blindly fumbled inside it, and pulled out a paper cone. Tightly rolled with top ends folded and tucked inwards to keep their cache from spilling, it was one of the six paper cones inside – one for each school day of the week, including the half-day on Saturdays.

Dr. Sheila Mehta, known as "Sheila Aunty," to all the children in the building, heard the clank made by the opening and closing of a steel lid in her kitchen. She glanced at the clock. Yes, it was about time, she thought with satisfaction, putting her book aside immediately. As she rose from her reading chair, she heard a familiar voice hollering, "Thanks, Sheila Aunty!"

She smiled indulgently as she walked towards the window, wanting a word with her visitor.

Meanwhile, his mission accomplished, eleven-year-old Shaamil, paper cone in hand, turned to hop off the stool that the building watchman was told to let him use, and also to ensure he didn't fall off it.

Questionable as this practice appeared, it suited them. How else could Shaamil take one of the snack cones that Sheila Aunty kept specially for him every afternoon when he returned from school? How else could she ensure that she could give him the snacks when she was out and about? How else could they keep their everyday routine otherwise? This routine established a couple of years ago when the aroma of her fried peanuts had stopped him dead in his tracks outside the same kitchen window, truly served them perfectly.

"It smells so yummy!" he had declared, taking a deep breath dramatically, his eyes closing in pleasure. Sheila Aunty had laughed. Then, quickly rolling up a paper cone, she had filled it with the chevdo she had just finished making, and handed it to him through the window.

A week later, she was at the window again when he was returning from school.

"Shaam?" she had called him and asked, "Would you like a snack?"

At his eager nod, she handed him another paper cone filled with chakris this time.

Soon enough it became an everyday occurrence, and Sheila Aunty started keeping a container of "Snack Cones" near the window for him, and with a little help of the watchman, he could help himself even if she wasn't around.

*****

"Wait, wait, Shaam!" she called , hurrying to the window before he jumped off the stool.

"Ya, Sheila Aunty?" Shaamil asked.

"How was the math test? And oh, before I forget, please tell Mona..." then correcting herself, she said, "tell Mom to call me when she can, ok?"

"The math test was easy-peasy, and okay, I will tell her, but today is Tuesday, and so ..." Shaamil attempted to explain, but she interrupted him. "Of course, the test wasn't hard for you. You are a clever, clever boy!! Yes, yes, I know it's Tuesday. That's why, that's exactly why I am asking you to ask her. I know she has hospital rounds today. And another thing. If you finish up your science project by 5 pm, you're welcome to come by to help make more cookies for the party," she added.

It didn't occur to Shaamil to question how and why everyone in the building knew everyone else's schedule and the smallest of life events, including school submissions. There was nothing odd about it. Just like the fact that his mom and Sheila Aunty were very close friends, even though they were both very different types of doctors, even though Mom was a pediatrician, and Sheila Aunty had a PhD in literature and taught English at St. Andrews College, some things were simply what they were. He still remembered how he had learned the difference between his mom's career and Sheila Aunty's, though he was probably only in kindergarten or in first grade at the time.

"If you are a doctor, you help people... you help people fight a tummy ache or maybe a headache, right?" he had asked.

"Right!" Sheila Aunty had always considered his questions seriously.

"So, Sheila Aunty? What do you help people fight?"

"I help them fight ignorance," Sheila Aunty had replied immediately, her hands curled up in a fist like a boxer, never lost for words when someone needed an explanation.

"Ig-Igno...?" he had asked, wide-eyed, giving up on this new word. "Does that hurt?"

"Ig-no-rance."Sheila Aunty had sounded it out in three clipped syllables, but with a chuckle. "It means that someone needs to know more, to learn more," she had clarified, "and yes, it absolutely hurts! Ignorance hurts us, but usually, it does not harm children, especially if they read a lot and learn to ask questions," she had assured him, her eyes twinkling. "But maybe if you are a lazy learner, you may get infected!"

That had been five years ago, but both Shaamil and Sheila Aunty and everyone else still remembered it.

"Don't forget to ask your mummy to call me!" she reminded him. "Tell her it's about the Christmas party."

"Oh, okay, I will tell her!" Shaamil responded, leaping off the stool and heading to the elevator to take him to his fifth-floor home, where either or both his aayah, Janki- bai and Zaverlal Maharaj, their general housekeeper and cook, would be waiting.

His mind was still on the Christmas party that Sheila Aunty and his mom planned together for all the children in the building, when the elevator doors opened. He turned left towards his door, but just then, he heard his name called out from his right.

“Shaamil? Home, are you?” a reedy voice asked him.

“Ji, yes, Dadi-ma!” he said, looking up at the oldest resident of the building, shuffling towards the elevator with a covered plate, the delicious aroma of cooked onions, tomatoes, ginger, and spices wafting around her. Shaamil took in the rich smells, breathing deeply, without meaning to. Just as Sheila Aunty shared her snacks with him for no good reason, Dadi-ma was bringing food for Aadit-bhaiya, no doubt!

“Good, good! Make sure you are done with your homework before going down to make more cookies!” she reminded him.

“Ji, Dadi-ma,” he answered.

She was not his grandma, but was “Dadi-ma” to all because everyone in the building considered her such, and she behaved as such. Demanding respect and instant subservience, she made it clear to all that her age gave her an indisputable right to advise and interfere and foist her company as well as her comments on anyone she chose.

On one such mission today, she pressed the elevator button for the third floor, heading to the Shah’s place with a bowl of chole in hand and a whole lot of scoldings on the tip of her tongue. After all, it was Tuesday, and Dadi-ma felt compelled to bring a dish for the Shah's younger son Aadit, only because Bharti Shah insisted on cooking different dals based on the day of the week!

No matter the state of the world - unless it was a religious holiday, a birthday, or an anniversary - Bharti ran her kitchen like clockwork. It was always whole amaranth lentils with garlic on Saturdays, a yellow dal on Sundays, a white-ish dal on Mondays, a red dal on Tuesdays, a green dal on Wednesdays, and so on.

Why would Bharti place more importance on some sort of astrological recommendation over her family's choices? Simply ludicrous, she thought, the idea never failing to exasperate Dadi-ma ever since she had heard that Aadit hated red dal and refused to eat it. Bharti had attempted to explain to Dadi-ma several times that she did serve other things that Aadit ate, but to no avail! Dadi-ma insisted on delivering a protein-rich dish that Aadit liked or would condescend to eat, along with a piece of her mind for Bharti every Tuesday.

As far as Dadi-ma was concerned, it was wrong! No matter Bharti's reasons, Dadi-ma couldn't wrap her brain around the explanation. She wouldn't. Why would anyone base their household's menu based on some age-old ideas of which dal to cook on different days of the week? "Thank goodness I am still alive to right such wrongs," she'd say to herself.

Dadi-ma rang the bell and when the house-servant Sita opened the door, she strode in as though it was her own house. Finding Bharti on the phone, she sat down on the couch facing her, and unabashedly listened in on the conversation.

"That's wonderful, Beta!" Bharti was saying, her smile widening so that it slipped into her voice, and raised it up a few decibels.

Dadi-ma gestured, "What happened?" with her hands, asking her to share the news, and Bharti nodded in response, but raised her own palm in a "Wait, wait!" motion. Then, after a couple more minutes of listening, she finally finished up her conversation.

"Who was it?" Dadi-ma demanded. "What is wonderful?"

"It was Aayush, Dadi-ma! Please bless him to ward off any evil eye from hindering his progress!" said a beaming Bharti. Then she turned to Sita-bai and ordered, "Please make tea for us."

"So, what is wonderful? Are you going to tell me, or wait until I completely lose my hearing?" Dadi-ma repeated, scolding her.

"Aayush was awarded a promotion and..." but before Bharti could complete her news, Dadi-ma put in her two bits.

"Arrey wah! Congratulations! We should welcome such sweet news with sweets! You must distribute pedas or some other treats to everyone in the building...but wait, how much of a pay raise did he get?" she asked, neither batting an eyelid nor displaying the tiniest tinge of hesitation in her voice.

"Oh no, I forgot to ask!" Bharti was not lying.

Undeterred, the older lady commanded, "Well, call him now and ask him, so we know whether or not to celebrate in a big way."

Just then, Bharti's nineteen-year-old daughter Diva walked in. Finding Dadi-ma seated right in the middle of the sofa, a fleeting frown crossed her pretty face, but she quickly concealed it. She greeted the older woman with a hurried, “Namaste, Dadi-ma,” and a quick bow because, like it or not, she still had to be respectful to someone older than her, especially a senior citizen. Her parents expected no less from her - her dad often reminded her that no matter how the other person behaved, “You must show them you are a lady.” But beyond basic courtesy, Diva wasn’t willing to entertain Dadi-ma in any way.

“Mom, I am going to wash up and then go to Sheila Aunty’s to help her make cookies for the Christmas party,” she said, and escaped from the room, bristling at the reason for Dadi-ma’s weekly visits.

“Tell Sheila to make more of the marzipan ones,” Dadi-ma said to Diva’s retreating back, completely oblivious to Diva’s exasperation.

*****

Diva could not abide the old lady, her opinions, her meddling ways, or even her presence for the most part, and privately had labeled Dadi-ma “a crusty old biddy.” Why couldn’t Dadi-ma be like Sheila Aunty? Sheila Aunty was kind and caring, she treated everyone with equal respect, even inviting the children of the building watchman and janitor to the Christmas party. Dadi-ma was still stuck in the past, and what was worse, she played favorites!

It was as clear as day that Dadi-ma was very affectionate to the children, but she changed her tune once they were in their adolescent years. Then she suddenly became stricter with the girls, holding them to a higher standard of conduct than the boys.

Old-fashioned as it was, Dadi-ma's reasoning was simple and, again, offered unsolicited: "Diva will marry and will live with her in-laws, " she'd say with a dramatic flourish, poking the air with her bony index finger at every word. "She'll have to adapt to the traditions and tastes of her in-laws' home. She can't get in the habit of not wanting to eat this or demanding that, or she'll be shedding tears every day! Tears as big as berries. Mark my words! Aadit, on the other hand, will get a wife who will cook what he wants, so he doesn't have to eat anything he doesn't like!"

To make her prejudices even more obvious, Dadi-ma made it a point to bring a dish of something that Aadit liked every Tuesday, but she'd never think to send anything for Diva. Not once, not ever! That felt like Dadi-ma was rubbing salt on a weekly basis after making such cutting remarks.

But Diva's true resentment began that day three years ago when she had overheard Dadi-ma telling her mom with a sniff, "Your Diva is supposedly fasting on Mondays, but she probably guzzles milkshakes and stuffs herself with ice-creams, nuts and fruits. Isn't that what the Swiggy guys deliver to your doors every Monday?"

What a busybody! Really? She tracks Swiggy deliveries, too? thought Diva, about to explode in fury. Doesn't everyone fast with fruits and milk and sugar? It's not as though she's paying for my Swiggy orders, or bringing me anything I like! What is Dadi-ma's problem? She wished she hadn't asked that question even to herself because she soon found out. Aaargh!

"All these young girls fasting on the pretext of pleasing Lord Shiva, but really so that He can grant them good husbands," Dadi-ma had plowed on, though no one had asked her. "I wasn't born yesterday. And Diva better watch out. Even with those beautiful doe-eyes, it won't do her any good if she ends up being as plump as her mother!"

"Really?" Diva fumed during dinner that day. "Why doesn't she mind her own business, Mom? She's like a dark cloud...constantly raining on everyone's parade with her advice. Who needs it? One of these days I'm going to tell her off!"

"Calm down, Beta," her dad patted her hand. "We don't disrespect our elders."

"But, but..." Diva sputtered, "why? Why? Why is it her business to comment on anything and everything?"

"That's their way...this is what the older generations faced while they were growing up and so that's what they know to do. Don't take it to heart," her mom said gently. "She's not a bad sort. Really."

"Really, Mom? You don't care that she called you 'plump'? Why is she excused for not having a filter, but we still have to toe the line? I never hear her commenting on any men. Doesn't she see her own son's potbelly? Just because he's a man, he's allowed to be as fat as he wants, right? How backward! She has some nerve!" Diva was still seething.

But her mom just smiled and shook her head. "There's no point in railing against something that we can't change. And trust me, she cares. You'll understand her when you get older."

Well, Diva was three years older now. She still couldn't fathom her mom's meek acceptance of such offensive comments. However, she had heard plenty of murmurings that were quickly muted when she'd come upon them suddenly, and Diva had heard enough broken bits to piece it together over that time.

Apparently, when Mukherjee uncle couldn't control his 72-year-old drunken dad from hitting his mom, he had rushed to Dadi-ma in the middle of the night.

Dadi-ma had thrown a shawl over her nightie, swept down the steps like a force of nature, and had stood between the old man and his wife.

"Move over, you, you... old witch!" the senior had slurred, but Dadi-ma had stood there, resolute.

"I'm warning you, I will beat you up, too!" he had repeated a few times, but Dadi-ma did not budge.

By then, a small crowd of building residents had gathered on the second floor, watching the drama unfold. When he began teetering towards her, Jessica, the daughter-in-law, came forward with a couple of men, but Dadi-ma raised her hand and waved them away imperiously, still standing there between Senior Mukherjee uncle and his wife.

Finally, blubbering and stumbling, he had gone into his bedroom, and slammed the door closed. Dadi-ma then calmly walked to the door and latched it from the outside.

"Do not open this door till I return in the morning!" she had commanded. "No matter how much he yells or threatens, let him stew in his hangover. I'll come by and sort him out."

Apparently, she had done just that.

The next morning, marching in with one of her cronies' grand-nephews, a police inspector who unlocked the door, she went inside the room, closed the door and scared him enough so there were no repeat incidents.

Reflecting on it now, Diva sighed. Well, all right, she conceded. Dadi-ma bore no ill will, and probably even cared for everyone, underneath her annoying and meddlesome ways. And yes, Dadi-ma truly believed that she was minding everyone's business because she considered everyone in the building to be her business. And yes, Dadi-ma's heart was in the right place even though her words and actions were not.

As she was slipping her feet into her chappals, she heard Dadi-ma say, “A promotion! My blessings to Aayush. May he rise to greater heights of success!” It was followed by, “Diva, tell Sheila the good news. She will be so happy! After all her help with his English essays, she deserves to know.”

“Ji, Dadi-ma,” Diva replied at the door, but before she could close it behind her, she heard Dadi-ma say, ”Now, how about we order a box of pedas for each household in the building? It is good for young boys like Shaamil to have proper models to emulate, not just the cricketers that these young kids idol worship. Youngsters also need to see how their successes are a cause of pride and rejoicing for all of us...”

Sparking the Story

One of the first unpleasant things that strikes a tourist visiting India besides an overwhelming stink in the air, is the teeming population – masses of people spilling out on the streets, out of trains, and into each other's spaces. So, the poor air quality is mainly due to the sheer number of humans cramped in the country.

Approximately 1.4 billion people live in a land with an area of 169,219 square miles, which is 3,345 feet per person. Not too bad, anyone would think, until we compare it to America, which has about 317,814 feet per person, and realize that the stratosphere or an ozone layer can only do so much. But along with India's lack of general space, let alone personal space, it may explain, if not excuse, the non-existence of personal boundaries or the concept of personal space. A meagre 2.4 percent of the world surface area housing a whopping 17.7 percent of the world population leaves little room for many of the niceties that call for space!

Even so, it is startling to find the extent to which neighbors will ask you the most personal of questions, offer you unasked advice, and share their unfiltered opinions. In fact, if you are a senior citizen, you can also have carte blanche to say whatever you want, with no regard to anyone's sensitivities, and body-shaming isn't off limits. By the same token, as annoying or even infuriating as it is to have everyone mind your business, neighbors do take care of you when you are ill, bring you food, or send it over with their servants just because it's your favorite dish or the giver wants to share a special treat. In short, nosiness and neighborliness go hand in hand.

A social custom to note is that children or young adults are expected to address friends of their parents and other adults of their parents' age as "Uncle" or "Aunty" or "Dadi-Ma" and "Dada-ji" if older, as long as they belong to the same social class. However, adults working blue-collar jobs, no matter their age, will usually be called by their first names.

As far as "fasting" for a religious purpose goes, Hinduism allows for as much leeway or limitation as permitted by the belief system followed by individuals or their families or sects. For instance, in some families "fast-approved items" may be eaten all day and may include fruits, dairy, potatoes in any form (potato chips, too), and so on, while others may adhere to a different regimen on fasting and non-fasting days. Also, people fast on a specific day of the week to overcome any of life's challenge or accomplish any achievable goal, for example, fasting on Mondays to please Lord Shiva who can grant "a good husband."

The tradition of cooking certain dals on certain days was followed at a time when astrology and ayurveda prevailed, though very few Indians know of it now. My sisters and I remember that mummy followed this tradition of yesteryear in a limited way; for example, she cooked dals that served as laxatives only on Saturdays. We also remember our maternal grandmother saying that such-and-such a lentil was cooked because it was a certain day of the week.

Meanwhile, hard as it may be to believe, the beginning of the story is based on the heartwarming fact that for many years, my mother-in-law always remembered to keep a tin of savories near a specific window, so that our family friends' son in the next apartment could grab a handful or two on his way home from school.

2.

Somewhere in India

, God has many forms

Background information / Vocabulary:

Dada-ji - Respected Grandfather

Ganesh - one of the many names of the elephant-headed Hindu God worshipped first in any religious ceremony

Jai-dev - God of victory, and in a prayer, a salutation conveying "Victory of the divine" to honor Lord Ganesh

hangry - being irritable due to hunger

tiffin boxes - bagged lunch or snacks in plastic containers or bags

Pandavas - The five brothers and legendary heroes central in the epic battle, "The Mahabharata," where the setting has been interpreted as an allegory for the struggles of human life in Hindu culture. During the battle, Lord Krishna's counsel to Arjuna, one of the brothers, comprises the holy text of the Hindus, "The Bhagavad Gita"

Hanuman - a deity in a monkey-like form and the devoted follower of Lord Rama, whose exploits, including leaping over an ocean, are described in "The Ramayana," also a sacred text for practicing Hindus

Sita - a Hindu goddess and the consort of Lord Rama

Mount Meru - a sacred mountain around which the world revolves, whose foothills are the Himalayas according to Hindu and Buddhist mythology

Draupadi - the daughter of King Drupad, she served as the common-law wife to the Pandavas, but committed to only one of the five brothers per year

Devi – a word for Goddess in Sanskrit – the language of the Hindu scriptures

SHERU'S TAIL WAS SWISHING like a slow pendulum. Familiar with the morning routine, he was waiting patiently, periodically shifting his adoring gaze from one face to the other. All was well in his world, his body language proclaimed.

"Jai dev, jai dev..." prayed Satyajit Bedekar. He had already lit a small wick soaked in ghee with a matchstick, and then used its flickering flame to light an incense stick. As the thin, sooty swirl of incense smoke disappeared into the air, diffusing the scent of sandalwood across the room, he continued to pray — palms clasped, eyes closed, and head bowed at the carved, miniature wooden temple mounted on the dining-room wall. Seated at the dining table laden with everyone's choice of breakfast foods along with airtight containers of snacks and cereals, his grandchildren remained respectfully silent, but no sooner did he open his eyes, both clamored for his attention.

"Dada-ji, I'm waaaiiiting....!" wailed Nirvaan.

"Now, will you tell me?" asked fourteen-year-old Alia, just as impatient though she was almost twice as old as her brother. "Pleeease, Dada-ji?" she implored, reaching for the tall cereal container with Multi-grain Almond Clusters.

Satyajit Bedekar turned to his granddaughter with a twinkle in his eye, while his grandson whined, "Daaadaaajee! I am hungreee!"

Satyajit Bedekar, his smile hidden in his silver moustache and beard, patted his grandson's curly-haired head gently. Then he picked up the first toast out of the pop-up toaster with tongs, laid it aside to cool, and teased, "Are you sure you're hungry? Didn't you eat just ten hours ago?"

Next, instead of buttering the toast, he opened the bin of dog food and poured a measured cupful into Sheru's bowl. The German Shepherd's tail was now thumping faster on the tiled floor, but he waited till he was told "Food is served, Sheru" before he lunged for it. Sheru was still the most patient of his charges by far, no question about it, thought Satyajit Bedekar in amusement. Then returning to his Grandfather or "Dada-ji" mode, he reached for the next two toasts still in the toaster. His movements on autopilot, he first slathered butter from edge to edge. While the butter melted on the golden warm toast, he applied a trace of strawberry jam on it, then placed a slice of cheese on each of them before sliding them onto Nirvaan's plate.

Nirvaan reached for it right away, and bit into his toast, though he knew that Dada-ji would not eat his breakfast until Sheru's needs were met. As expected, Dada-ji gave the first toast to the dog since it was no longer too hot, and then began to fill the dog's water bowl carefully to avoid spilling, though Sheru would soon splatter it around the dish, anyway.

"Dada-ji?" prompted Alia. "Is this test going to be very hard?"

"No, no! No, I promise...but let me think..." Dada-ji closed his eyes for a couple of seconds, stroking his bearded chin dramatically, as though summoning some magical insight. Then he nodded, opened his eyes, and predicted, "There's not a thing to worry about! You will find this math test to be mostly simple. Just don't rush while solving your fifth problem and the second-last question..." and after a brief pause, "and you WILL ace the test!"

Alia stared at him, mouth open in hopeful disbelief, forgetting to chew her cereal for a few seconds.

"You're just saying that to make me feel less nervous, aren't you? Admit it. You said something like that for my last test, too!" she accused, pointing her spoon at her grandfather.

"Alia, Alia. Look at me. It will be all right. Wasn't I right the last time? Did you not get a 98 out of 100? Did you not mess up on the polynomial problem alone?" he questioned.

*****

This was how it had been with Satyajit Bedekar and his grandchildren, even when his wife Niyati had been alive. He was the calm center of their whirlwind mornings, the softest spot of their hardest days, a partner-in-crime during their occasional nighttime raids of the pantry, and sometimes, a Genie with magical prophecies. With his son and daughter-in-law being busy physicians, he had been the one to play with the kids and to turn for homework help, too. He had so much more patience now, and he would tutor his grandchildren in a way that their parents didn't have the time for, in a way that he never had the time for when his own children were young.

Slow down...one fine morning, you'll wake up and suddenly find you are seventy-five years old like me, he wanted to tell his son and his daughter-in-law more often than he already did.

Now he knew that there was nothing better than time spent with loved ones. Now he also wished that he'd made the time to enjoy his own children while they were growing up. Now he made it a point to remind himself that life was even shorter than when he was thirty-five, and certainly too short to waste regretting the past. What mattered was that he was lucky enough to be given a second chance and to be around those who mattered the most — his grandchildren. Embracing his new role wholeheartedly, he had found that his grandchildren filled his days with the kind of boundless and heart-bursting love he had not known to exist in this world.

"Dadaji, why do you always feed Sheru first?" asked Nirvaan, as he reached for his second toast, interrupting his grandfather's train of thought.

Nirvaan's observational skills had recently improved, thanks to D'Souza Ma'am, his third-grade teacher, who reminded the class daily to notice their surroundings, to be curious, and to ask thoughtful questions.

"Because we brought him home, and he depends on us to feed him. If we don't, he may feel sad. And, it's really not fair because he can't find his own food like animals in the wild or the strays who live on the streets do," answered their grandfather, filling up the dog's water bowl again.

"Sad, and maybe hangry...like me?" asked Nirvaan.

"Sheru is a good boy. He doesn't get 'hangree', but as I was saying, Sheru depends on us. He cannot hunt or buy his own food, and so he is our responsibility. Our dogs are a part of our family, and how we treat our dogs shows the kind of humans we are," said their grandfather.

Then, almost as an afterthought, he added, "Some believe that the way we treat dogs can even determine our entry into heaven."

"You mean that besides a god with an elephant head, and a god with a monkey head, we also have a god who takes the form of a dog?" asked Alia. "Like Sirius? You know, from Harry Potter? Or maybe like Cerberus? Except that maybe the one we have watches the gates of heaven instead of hell...is that what they believe?"

"No, not like that. Sirius Black could only turn into a black wolfhound and Cerberus had no shape-shifting powers ," replied her grandfather, his eyebrows raised in recognition, as he often read books they recommended to him, "whereas many of our gods can transform themselves into more than just one or two forms. We don't have time for a story right now. But if you want, I'll tell you about it on our way to school."

"Yay, a story!" exclaimed Nirvaan.

But before Satyajit Bedekar could remind his grandson that the story would have to wait until they were on their way to school, they heard morning prayers blasting on loudspeakers from the Ganesha temple behind their home. As usual, the chants, accompanied by the clanging of bells and the beating of drums, prompted an instant flurry of activity.

Nirvaan chugged down his milk, Alia pushed back her chair and rushed to her room, Dada-ji drank up the last of his tea and stood up, and Sona, their cook, hurried out from the kitchen, handing everyone their own tiffin boxes. Sheru, not to be outdone, was suddenly in everybody's way.

The prayers at the temple lasted about four minutes, and these served as their alarm clock, their cue, to get moving. If they all managed to get out of the door before it ended, and that included their mom, who would leave for her clinic across the street, no one would be late.

"Bye, Nino, bye, Lia," their mom called, using their nicknames, "have a great day at school! All the best on your math test, Lia. And Nirvaan, eat the crust of your toast, too, and do NOT forget to take your history homework again! Mrs. D'Souza took off five points last time because you gave it to her a day late. If you submit it after the Christmas break, you'll just get a zero! Oh, and there's a bag for each of you with small Christmas treats for your teachers on the foyer table," she added, at the door, ready to head to her clinic.

Alia ran to give her mom a quick hug, while Nirvaan and his grandfather exchanged a conspiratorial look.

"Did you hear me?" their mom asked again. "Eat the crust as well!"

"Ya, Mom, I heard you! And okaaayyy, I will eat the crust," he said. His grandfather waggled his eyebrows at him, but then pretended to look away when Nirvaan slipped the crust to Sheru, who had been slavering right there for it, his stare unwavering. Silently and swiftly, Sheru caught the crust and swallowed it down smoothly—it was a catch-crunch-and-down-the-hatch operation of stealth that took less than 5 seconds.

Then, Nirvaan wiped his milk moustache and hands on the madras-printed hand towel, hurried to grab his backpack, and put on his shoes.

Alia, waiting at the door with a leash in her hand, yelled, “Sheru, here!”

Sheru ran around the room for a few excited zoomies before coming to stand beside Alia so she could put his leash on. That accomplished, while Sheru’s tail whirred fast, she grabbed the walking stick to beat back the stray dogs they would definitely encounter along the way.

Three minutes of scrambling later, they were ready to leave for their short walk to school.

“The story, Grandpa?” reminded Nirvaan, as soon as they had stepped outside their gates.

“Yes, so about your question: Do we have a god who can assume the form of a dog? Yes, we absolutely do. Our gods have different shapes, distinct faces, and also unique powers to remind us that the Almighty lives in everything and everywhere... and that’s why we must care for every bit of creation. All forms are sacred, all are divine—human, animal, and every bit of Nature.”

“Everything? Is there a god in the wind?” Nirvaan asked with a sparkle in his eyes.

“Sure, we do...because nothing moves without God! Our God of the Winds is Vaayu or Pavan. He is the life breath of the world, and the messenger of the Gods,” Grandfather answered. “The God of Winds is also the father of Hanuman. Remember how he flew over the ocean to save Goddess Sita?”

“Ohhh!” Nirvaan processed the detail and was about to kick a pebble, but he gently rolled it aside, and asked, “Is there a God in stones, too?”

“Not just in stones, but all minerals. In Hindu mythology, Kuber is in charge of all precious metals, all rocks and jewels that lie under and over the ground, and treasures in general.” replied Dada-ji.

“And, and, and, what about...what about?” Nirvaan’s eyes searched around their surroundings.

Alia held up her hand. “Stop, stop, Nino! Let Dada-ji finish the story. Otherwise, I’ll be thinking about it all day at school!”

Satyajit smiled at Alia. “There are a few myths, but the most well-known one is about a dog in one tale of the

Pandava brothers, five of our bravest legendary heroes. At the end of their lives, it was a dog, not any other animal, that accompanied them, following them on their final journey. As the myth goes, when Yudhishthira with his four younger brothers, and their wife Draupadi were trudging up Mount Meru far above the Himalayas to reach the heavens, one by one, all his brothers and wife died, but the dog stayed at his heels the entire way.

When Yudhishthira finally reached the last gates on earth, he found Indra, the God of the Heavens, Lightning, and Thunder, waiting there in his flying chariot. 'Welcome, Yudhishthira,' Indra said. 'You may step into my chariot, for you are valiant and virtuous, but I'm afraid your dog can't accompany you inside. He has done nothing to deserve paradise.

Yudhishthira bowed and said, 'Thank you for the honor, my Lord. But this dog has struggled to stay by my side — over treacherous paths, through terrible winds, and in the icy cold. He has made it all the way here. A dog is supposed to be faithful, and surely he has proved himself, and so, hasn't he earned the right to enter, too?'

'Yudhishthira, I will not argue with you, nor will I allow the dog to ascend to the heavens with you,' Indra replied firmly.

'Then I must respectfully decline your invitation, my Lord. I cannot abandon him after his loyalty to me, not even for an eternity in heaven,' said Yudhishthira, joining his palms and bowing his head in apology.

Indra was silent. He looked into Yudhishthira's eyes for a few long seconds and asked, 'Is this your final answer? Are you rejecting the promises of heaven for a dog?'

'Please forgive me, my Lord,' replied Yudhishthira. 'I mean no offence...'

But no sooner had he uttered the words, when the dog suddenly transformed into the God of Dharma—the God who upholds order and moral principles to keep the universe organized and running.'' Dada-ji explained.

"Whoa!" interjected Nirvaan. "Ree-ally?"

"Yes, Yudhishthira was stunned, too," said Dada-ji, and added, "Then, Indra said, 'You have passed your last test. You have proved yourself to be noble in life and also kind and caring of all creatures. You deserve to enter the heavens.'

Shimmering with power, the God of Dharma also blessed him, saying, 'You did not abandon a faithful companion, not even for heaven. For that, your name will always be associated with righteousness!'

And so, do you see? Dogs are part of our mythology, and how you value their loyalty can decide whether or not you can enter heaven!'" said their grandfather, just as the school gates came into view.

Suddenly, Nirvaan stopped, remembering the history notebook he'd left on the dining table. "Oh, no! I forgot my history homework again!" he cried.

"Don't look at me! I have a math test first thing this morning," said Alia, and shook her head in exasperation. "Oh, well, Mom will be mad as hell, and your teacher will..."

"Dada-ji, I will...I will get double hell today," Nirvaan said, his voice wobbly, imitating his sister's words, "from Mrs. D'Souza AND Mom! The school bell will ring any time now and, and with the Christmas break starting tomorrow..."

"No, no...Look at me, it'll be alright.... no one is getting any hell," said Dada-ji, placing his hands on his grandson's shoulders. Outwardly calm, he felt something clamping his heart when he saw Nirvaan's lower lip tremble a bit. He also felt the same indescribable scraping in his chest and the weakness in his legs whenever his grandkids experienced the smallest of tumbles or suffered from the mildest of fevers.

"But..but..." protested Nirvaan. Yet when he looked up to meet his grandfather's steady gaze, the twisting squirm in his tummy was gone. Dada-ji always made things better, he knew that.

Meanwhile, even as Satyajit Bedekar was figuring out how to help Nirvaan, he was well aware that he couldn't protect his children and grandchildren, or save them from their stresses or suffering forever. Someday, he would not be around. That thought made it momentarily hard to swallow. But that day was not here yet. Not today, at any rate, he decided, though he broke into the slightest of sweats, which had nothing to do with the cool morning air. He knelt down by the side of the road, so he was eye to eye with Nirvaan, and resting his hands gently on his shoulder, reassured him in a steady voice.

“Nirvaan, go on. Go to your classroom. Go give the Christmas treats to the other teachers...No wait!” Dada-ji said, struck by an idea. “Nirvaan, give me that bag of treats. I will return right away and hand it to Ms. Vakharia in the school office, but I will staple it close. Your history notebook will be inside it, okay? Look for it under the gifts. Sheru and I will walk home as fast as I can, and then I’ll come by with the bag. I will tell Ms. Vakharia or the others in the office that you forgot your Christmas treats for the staff, and it will be all good,” Dada-ji assured him. “We’ll fast-walk right back, okay? Trust me, it will all be good.”

Heart thumping a little faster than his doctor would have liked, Satyajeet Bedekar waited until Nirvaan entered the school gates. Then he turned around to head home at a brisk pace with no other thought than to relieve his grandson’s worry. Meanwhile, Sheru had heard “walk” and “good“ more than once, and all was well in his world. As they walked back, Sheru’s tail was swishing like a slow pendulum.

Sparking the Story

"Joint families" are still a normal way of life in India, and so it is common to see three and sometimes four generations living under the same roof. Also, noise pollution, as presented in the story, is rampant – prayers and chants blast at top volumes over loudspeakers in mosques and temples at their chosen times of the day; noise ordinances come into effect only after 11 pm in most parts of the country, and even then, these are imposed only if someone complains. In short, all the holidays of many religions are celebrated with great fervor and greater noise, and the loudspeakers keep booming on and on until someone calls the police.

It is also true that India is home to about 33 million deities. The learned devotee will explain that there is really only one God and the various faces and forms have been made so that it's easy for the masses to understand that there is a God in every part of creation. Some will compare them to the Greek or Egyptian pantheon of gods, goddesses, and demigods, where each deity embodies a unique or a shared supernatural power.

Many others will seek to explain this staggering number by comparing the universe to a large corporation, where Lord Krishna, believed to be the supreme being or the CEO, has assigned different powers to different beings to manage the different areas of creation and own the ability to manifest into different entities—the wind, the oceans, the trees, the mountains, and even into birds, beasts, and bugs. For example, Goddess Saraswati oversees the seeking of knowledge, Goddess Durga represents fierce maternal powers, Lord Yama handles death, Lord Surya is in charge of the sun, Bhramari Devi is the goddess of insects, especially bees, Garuda is a divine personification of courage in an eagle-like form, and so on.

Lastly, and importantly, it must be noted that these different gods often have overlapping authorities or specializations, and thus, Shiva and Kali are both deities in charge of destroying the evil on earth, besides being designated other minor duties. Similarly, Ganesh and Laxmi both share the responsibility of dispensing wealth and wisdom. For those who hold this viewpoint that God is in the business of keeping creation going, 33 million different gods to ensure that every facet of the universe works efficiently sounds perfectly reasonable.

3.

Somewhere in India

, this is how birthdays are often celebrated

Background information / Vocabulary:

Ben or Buhen - a suffix added to a name as a term of respect for women who are older or in a higher economic or professional status, literally translating to “sister”

Gujarati - one of the 22 official languages of India

Go-fer - an informal term for an employee who is hired for all the smallest of errands; a contraction of the words “go for,” it is a blue-collar job that involves going for this or that

“VIPIN,” I GREETED with a smile. I had been reading in the living room, when I saw the front door open and his tanned face peeking in. He smiled courteously in recognition, bowing his head slightly, closing the door behind him carefully.

All his efforts at a silent, circumspect entry were pointless, because Parle-G went berserk as usual. Belying his senior years, the yellow lab cried-yelped and circled around Vipin for attention, even though Vipin was fondly rubbing the top of Parle-G's head and around his ears with both hands, repeating, "Good morning, Parle-G! Good morning!" several times.

Only after these daily formalities were completed did Vipin slip off his shoes, adding his own pair to the line of other slippers, sandals, and shoes on the side of the threshold, and then padded onto the shiny, tiled floor. Even with his socks on, he was careful to avoid stepping on the Jaipur carpet, with its intricate pattern in pomegranate-maroon, cream, and lapis-blue.

Parle-G immediately went to work, sniffing Vipin's shoes thoroughly one at a time, then ambled off to his bedding in the foyer. He'd had enough excitement, his "humpff" seemed to say. Clumsily flopping down to rest his old bones, he laid his head down, ready to nap.

As I watched this meet-and-greet play I had seen during my earlier visits, I thought that something seemed to be a little different about Vipin. A yearly guest at my sister Sejal's home, everyone in her world knew me. But it was because we texted or chatted with each other almost daily, I was up-to-date with the times and troubles of all her household and some of their office help. Sejal was, undoubtedly, one of the most commendable managers I knew – she did not lose her "employees" or servants once they had worked with her for a handful of months. In fact, most of her current staff had been in her employment for over two decades. It was not, by no means, a small feat but she had instinctively implemented the best practices of our mum! Besides talking to them respectfully, which was not typical in most households, it was also because she was extremely generous and involved in their lives – paying their children's school fees, accompanying them to the Doctors' if they needed her support, and loaning them money for their pilgrimages or family weddings.

My rumination was interrupted when Vipin stopped in his stride, his eyes searching. One of Vipin's responsibilities as the head office peon and "go-fer" of the family business was to open and lock up the office, I knew. So, I had expected him to head towards the key organizer on the wall at the end of the hallway as usual. But he didn't, and instead waited hesitantly.

There was definitely something a little different about him, the thought kept niggling. Perhaps he's just getting older, I supposed, noticing the grey specks in his hair, and then remembered to ask about his family.

"How are you, all?" I asked in Gujarati, suddenly, recalling that his wife's cancer was in remission. "How is your wife?"

"Good, " he said. "She is much better, now that she's slowly gaining back her strength."

" ...And your children? How old are they now?"

"Sixteen, and the younger one is eleven," he said.

"So grown-up!" I responded, thinking of the gently-used clothes I still hadn't unpacked — my sons' hand-me-downs that I had brought back to India.

Clothes! That was it.

Vipin wasn't wearing the usual navy-blue office uniform, but a lemongrass-green shirt and newish jeans instead, both stiffly starched and pressed.

As he stood there somewhat hesitantly, I presumed he was looking for Sejal.

“Sejal-ben is in the kitchen,” I informed him in Gujarati, the state language spoken by all living in the area, heading there myself for a glass of water. He followed me, Parle-G trailing after him, his tail swaying.

“Vipin.” Sejal acknowledged him, but she did not comment on his attire either. Perhaps she knew the reason for his lapse in protocol.

In response, Vipin reached into his backpack with barely-suppressed excitement and handed her the biggest bar of dark chocolate to be found in the market. Costing over a hundred rupees, it was not a small amount for the reach of his pockets.

“It’s my Happy-birthday today!” he shared, speaking in Gujarati as usual, except for the words “Happy Birthday,” his eyes crinkling.

Ohhh, it’s his birthday today, I realized, amused at his phrasing just as realization dawned that besides a smattering of a few English words, Vipin’s world comprised mostly two languages – Gujarati and Hindi. This meant that all celebratory wishes are probably expressed in Gujarati or Hindi, and the word “happy” is probably the only occasion associated with birthdays. Ah, it dawned on me, he believes that “Happy” is an inseparable part of a birthday! How funny, how cute! The thought made me smile.

"Thank youuuu!" Sejal replied with a chuckle, seeing Vipin's obvious excitement. Looking at me, she explained, "Vipin buys me the biggest bar of my favorite chocolate, every year on his birthday," before she turned her attention back to him.

"So how old are you, today?" she asked, striding out of the kitchen to her bedroom, but still within earshot.

"Thirty-seven!" Vipin replied proudly, waiting near the kitchen entrance.

Almost immediately, Sejal returned and said, "Thirty-seven? Happy Birthday!! Oh, that's why the new clothes!"

Vipin drew another bar from his voluminous backpack.

"This is for Sir," he explained.

"Thank you, Vipin." Sejal smiled, taking the offered bar for her husband and putting it in the fridge. "I will give it to him later. Thank you! Now, I won't have to share my bar with him."

While Vipin and I chuckled at that, she fished out her wallet and handed him what seemed to be more than a couple of hundred rupees. As expected, her proffering brought forth the usual token protests of, “No, no ...you don’t have to give me anything.”

“Take it!” she urged gently.

Then she paused, suddenly remembering. "Wait...isn’t it your younger son’s birthday the day after yours? Tomorrow, right?” she asked.

Vipin nodded, smiling like an excited child who has spied not one but two rainbows that no one else seemed to have noticed yet.

“Yes,“ he nodded, his eyes sparkling, “it is his happy-birthday tomorrow!”

Sejal dug into her purse again and gave him three fifty-rupee notes.

“Here, buy him something he wants for his birthday,” she added, with a smile. Eleven-year-olds usually have a list.”

“No, Sejal-ben, not a list. This year, he wants a puppy,” Vipin shared. “A dog that’s the same color as our

Parle-G, I have been instructed," he added with a smile, nodding towards the old Golden Lab. "I will try to get him a puppy from the stray litter behind our colony."

Then, with nostalgia coating his words, he shook his head. "Today's children can ask for things on their birthdays. Not like when I was a boy. Nobody gave it a thought in those times. Nobody remembered it, not even my mom. It was just another day. No special food, no treats, and if we acted up, we were spanked as usual. But not anymore, now, things are different..." he continued, finally accepting the money.

Then, he went to the key organizer, picked up the keys, and turned towards the front door, a hint of a smile still lingering on his face. Parle-G rose from his bed and shuffled up to him for a goodbye pat. Vipin rubbed Parle-G's head a few times, murmuring, "I'll be back soon, okay? I'll see you in the evening, okay?"

Reaching the door, he checked with Sejal. "May I leave?" he asked, and only after hearing her say, "Sure," he slid on his shoes.

Quietly, he opened the door, and with his shoulders drawn back, Vipin headed out to a world that now held his happy birthday, too.

Sparking the Story

The lives of the poor and the privileged mostly run parallel in India, and yet are threaded together so closely at intermittent points that they are hard to separate. But even as their lives interweave, the inequities are obvious in their celebrations and sufferings. For instance, the rich will often mark their birthdays with as much giving as taking, especially children in pre-k through Grade 8.

Some people choose to donate generously in cash or kind to charities and to their household help, especially on milestone birthdays. However, until the last few decades, birthdays were not family celebrations among the poorer or blue-collar classes. Now it is apparent that most of them have learned and adopted these modern ways from their employers and Bollywood movies, and celebrate their own birthdays, too.

It is worthwhile to remember that since the cost of food, especially sweets, has always been high in India relatively, these treats are always accepted graciously. Employees of small businesses, having been served ice-cream or cakes to celebrate birthdays of their higher-ups or their employers' children, now find their own special day recognized similarly.

Many schools still offer special privileges to the birthday child. When I was a schoolgirl, it was a common custom for the birthday child to bring candy, sometimes even more treats, for all our 50-plus classmates as well as for all the teachers—the "Ma'ams" and "Sirs" who had taught us through the years. Even more exciting, the birthday children could pick one friend to accompany them to offer goodies to all their past instructors. And, if you were the chosen one, ahh, it was the icing on the cake! What an honor! You were the envy of your classmates because you were about to get a fun break - traipse around in the school hallways, perhaps even pocket an extra sweet -while they sweated away on their classwork, and it wasn't even your birthday!

Sadly, I don't remember giving any thought to the lack of birthday celebrations of our household servants in my childhood years. Even today, birthday celebrations are beyond the reach of tens of thousands of children and adults in India. But patterns are changed one stitch at a time, and it has been heartwarming to find that, in some households, the fabric of customs now includes their helpers' birthdays and considering them people worthy of celebration.

4.

Somewhere in India

, fine shopping is finer

Background information / Vocabulary:

Rupees - the monetary units used in India

Idli/Idlis - a steamed, savory cake/s made from a batter of fermented white rice and de-husked black lentils

Masala chai - black tea brewed with milk, sugar, and spices such as cardamom, cinnamon, ginger powder, powdered cloves, and pepper

Adaah - translates to adornment, beauty, and grace in Urdu

Kuhdum - translates to step or footstep in Hindi

I'M DREAMING, KATIE THOUGHT groggily, her hands instinctively covering her ears. What was all that screeching? How...? Where on earth was she?

Jetlagged and disoriented as she was, Katie somehow forced her eyelids to open. Looking around the unfamiliar room, she saw wall hangings portraying scenes with doe-eyed women in saris, peacocks, and trees, and suddenly sat up on a futon-type mattress. Just then, a couple of squawking parrots in a serious skirmish drew her gaze to the screened window.

Then she remembered.

She was in India!

Fully awake now, she could still hardly believe it herself. The thought of being in India for a whole three weeks before Esha's wedding still seemed like a dream!

*****

Esha had begged her for months to come over with variations of "Please, please, pretty please come, please help me cope with all the craziness before the wedding!"

Katie, too, was madly eager to visit India. Having grown up in Pittsburgh, Pennsylvania, she couldn't remember a time without some Indian friends or another. Throughout her school years, she had been invited to their homes for birthday parties and sleepovers, she had traveled to debate competitions and Science Olympiads with them, and she hadn't yet tasted any Indian dish she disliked, but that was it. She had never attended an Indian wedding, nor had she visited India, so she was beyond excited when everything fell into place!

Katie planned to spend three weeks with Esha and then three weeks after the wedding exploring the country with a premier tour company. She could barely wait to experience the Taj Mahal, Jaipur - the Pink City, the markets, the Gir National Park – the last natural habitat of the Asiatic lion, and more!

"Really? Yayyy! Tell me you're not kidding me, Kat!" Esha had squealed when she'd heard. "My last days of being a single lady with you!! Woo-hoo!"

Besties right from their freshman dorm years through graduation though Esha had grown up in India, they had done a lot of things together over four years. A lot of firsts. In fact, Katie had been the first to know when Esha had fallen for Ronak two years ago.

“He is the one, Kats...I just know it,” Esha had confessed after returning from India after the Christmas break of her junior year.

“Wait! What?" Katie had asked, wide-eyed. "Did your parents find you a match? Seriously? I’d never have thunk you’d go for an arranged marriage...”

“You thunk right!” Esha interrupted and chuckled, “thunk” being one of their inside jokes to refer to “Total Hunk”, not just a fun way to use the past tense of “think”. “Nope, no arrangement, though I’m pretty sure Mom is happy about it.”

Apparently, Ronak Shroff had been the best man at the wedding she had attended during that visit. That had been almost two years ago.

After that, Ronak had visited Esha the following summer because she was taking summer classes, now suddenly eager to finish up. He had also returned for her graduation. The more time she spent with the couple, the more Katie was convinced that he really was the right one for Esha-- decisive as much as she was dithering, calm as much as she was chaotic, and sociable as much as she could be shy among strangers. But all said and done, "R.S." or "Rupees" (her nickname for him because he converted every dollar amount to rupees or rupees into dollars over every purchasing decision) was a sweetheart, easy on the eye, and a word-smith to boot!

*****

Katie smiled as she arose from bed. It was going to be a blast. The marathon of the wedding preparations would begin today. She was accompanying Esha and her mom, who had instructed Katie to address her as "Parul Aunty" to help Esha select one of the many wedding attires - this time, a sari that Ronak's mom would buy for her for the wedding reception.

"Oh, that's nice...!" Katie had responded with a laugh.

"Well, the bride's family buys the wedding sari and jewelry because while she is supposedly leaving her parents' home, she still represents them," Parul Aunty explained, "and so we'll be buying Esha's wedding attire.

After the wedding, she stands for her in-laws' family and so..." her voice sounding a bit choked, "and so they outfit her in a way that best reflects them and it includes her footwear, too. Believe it or not, in olden times, the bride's family would send her off without any footwear," she added, attempting a teary chuckle, quickly grabbing a tissue to blow her nose, "so she doesn't run back home unless her in-laws give her chappals. Of course, now, that's just a fun custom."

"Mumma, please don't be sad..." Esha implored, her own eyes misty, hugging her mother from behind.

"Oh, I'm not sad. I know how lucky I am to have you nearby...but it seems you were five years old just the other day...and now you're going to be a bride..." Parul Aunty had said, before shooing them off to get dressed.

Weddings are so bittersweet, Katie thought, brushing her auburn hair, quickly deciding to tie it into a topknot. While mothers of brides across the world commonly made similar remarks, she didn't know about any Indian wedding traditions or customs, except the circling around a fire that she had seen in Bollywood movies.

As she checked herself in the mirror, she heard Parul Aunty calling them from the kitchen, "Girls, hurry, and come down right now. Breakfast is ready. You should NOT add coping with a hunger headache to the tasks at hand today!"

The girls sat down at the table laden with bowls of papaya and pomegranate, steaming idlis with tomato and coconut chutneys along with some cardamom shortbread cookies. After finishing up with a mug of masala chai, the girls quickly retouched their lipstick.

Soon all three were off, ready to shop for the reception sari at a specialty showroom and apparel store.

As the family driver Vishnu dropped them in front of an imposing store called "Adaah," Esha turned to her.

"Brace yourself, Kats. You are in for it — shopping for fine clothing here is not for wimps...more than likely, there will be enough good options to leave you dizzy!" Her palms swept out as though she was presenting an exhibition of sorts, leading her friend towards a showroom door. The entrance was manned by a uniformed guard sitting on a stool, who stood up from his chair right away, and opened the door for them, nodding courteously.

"What do you mean?" asked Katie, looking around wide-eyed, as she stepped into the air-conditioned store faintly perfumed with hints of a floral bouquet. The interior looked very shiny, complete with spotless mirrors stretching across the walls and ceiling, carved faux marble partitions to match the gleaming marble floors and mannequins in bejeweled and sequined brocades.

Esha murmured, "Wait ..." and just then a sales attendant asked Parul Aunty, "What can I show you today, Madam?"

"We are looking for a reception sari, but we are meeting someone here," explained Parul Aunty.

"Are you here to shop with Anjali ma'am?" he enquired politely. Then, seeing Parul Aunty nod, he said, "Please follow me," and ushered them further into the caverns of the store.

"So posh! But I don't get it. A sari is not like a wedding gown. I mean, any sari can be worn for many occasions, so can't you just check things out casually?" murmured Katie.

"Ooooh no, girl. You can't do that. Not for any formal finery!" semi-whispered Esha, as they were led through a door that opened up to a circular room divided into four sections.

Katie glanced around and saw that each section had pristine-white ottomans and sofas facing a low stage, which was manned by sales representatives. Beyond the stage, open shelves lined the walls and held folded and stacked clothing in transparent plastic bags, but way out of reach.

"There you are!" said Parul Aunty as she caught sight of a bunch of ladies. Katie was surprised. She hadn't expected a shopping entourage. But she saw an older lady who seemed to be well in her eighties as well as three other ladies, all staring at her curiously before she noticed Ronak's mom or "Moms" as he referred to her, whom she recognized from photographs and Facebook posts. Apparently, when Ronak was in Third Grade, he insisted that he should be allowed to name his parents just as they had named him. He then used words he had heard each of them say and thought "Doodads," was perfect for his gizmo-loving dad and "Cardamoms" suited his mom because it was her favorite mouth-freshener and she always carried a small box filled with that fragrant spice. However, these titles were soon whittled down to "Dads" and "Moms," and they stuck.

Feeling as though she were in a different era altogether, Katie lowered herself on one of the ottomans, speechless at the splendor and sparkle around her.

"Do you have something specific in mind? Color? Style?" she heard the sales attendant ask.

"No, not really...but I don't want this year's 'in' color. I don't want to wear the same colors that all the brides are wearing this season," Esha said hesitantly.

"Peach-Orange is IN, madam, and really, it is the best color for your fair skin!" he began his pitch. "But what is your price range?"

Katie knew well that bridal store consultants often cut to the chase with such questions, but its practicality usually ended up dialing down the buzz of shopping a bit. She turned to her friend, her brows raised.

Esha touched Katie's arm lightly, as Ronak's mom told him, "Show us a few options in different price ranges and don't waste everyone's time with cheap stuff." Hearing that, one of the sales attendants quickly took off to a deeper part of the store, while another pulled swaths and saris from different shelves.

Soon, the sales agents began unfurling sari after sari

- brocades, silks, chiffons, inlay work, beadwork, cutwork - the variety was dazzling, making a mountain of them on the stage.

Katie watched, mesmerized. This will take hours to fold, the thought came unbidden, as more saris were exhibited and extolled with enthusiasm.

When one of the sales attendants realized that Esha seemed to be favoring a couple of blue saris, he said, “We have some new items, though they are slightly more expensive than what we have seen so far, but absolutely unique - each, a masterpiece!”

“No, no...we don’t need to see that,” Esha demurred, the color rising in her cheeks.

“Memsahib, it doesn’t cost to look, “ he said, using the marketing spiel all clothing sales attendants use. You don’t have to buy anything! Just let me show you! What do you say, madam?” he turned to check with her mother-in-law.

“Sure, we can look,” replied Mrs. Shroff.

The man stepped away and returned in no time with five saris, all of them truly stunning.

Esha looked awed, but seemed unwilling to choose any of the beautiful pieces, perhaps because they came with astounding prices, too.

Fortunately, Mrs. Shroff had been watching Esha's expressions carefully, and said, "Would you open the light-blue one so we can see the work done on it?"

The sales attendant needed no more prompting, and he spread it out at once, even showing how the pleats and the border would look when worn. It was an ice-blue brocade with tiny gems in pink and gold.

"What do you think of this?" the matriarch among them asked Esha.

"It's beautiful, but..." Esha began.

"Do you like it? Is it something you'd like to wear?" asked Mrs. Shroff, gently.

"Yes, but I liked a few from the regular collection as well! This is a bit... this is too much to spend!" Esha protested. "I'm not sure if we should..."

"Let's call Ronak Sir and get his opinion, shall we?" interrupted the sales attendant.

Katie was puzzled. What was Ronak doing here?

But before she could utter a word, there he was, as real as the razzle-dazzle around her, accompanied by his younger brother Indrajeet and one of their cousins, Swaraj. He was looking at Esha, and as soon as she met his gaze, he raised one of his eyebrows slightly. Esha smiled in response and gave a tiny nod. Unlike Katie, she seemed to expect him to be there.

"What are you all doing here?" Katie asked.

"I'm here to shop for a sari!" he responded with a laugh.

"Great timing...how did you…?" Katie began, but he continued.

"Katie, we were waiting in the next room, watching the cricket match on TV over some soft drinks and snacks, staying out of your hair until you all narrowed the choices!" Ronak informed her. "There's no fine shopping without the approval of family and friends...and the groom."

"Yeah. That's how it's done. Trust me, it's a calculated move." Esha's face radiated a soft glow that bloomed every time she smiled at Ronak. "This way, the guys don't get impatient and rush us to make hasty decisions... or worse, start an argument and then everyone leaves in a huff," added Esha. "The men are requested to join us women only after the final decision has to be made to select from a handful."

"Yupp, we were being served a choice of refreshments!" Indrajeet affirmed.

Katie looked at the unfolding scene of smooth selling as the sales attendant lauded all the fine features of the three short-listed saris.

Ronak heard him out and then asked Esha softly, "Are you sure you like them equally?"

He was gazing at her with so much tenderness that a rush of happy tears sprang in Katie's eyes, and she blinked them away.

Esha's face crimsoned as she nodded shyly with the tiniest dip of her head, knowing that all eyes were upon them.

When Ronak asked, "Which of these seem really special to you?" she didn't respond right away, but before his mom and grandmamma said anything, the sales attendant jumped right in and said, "The ice-blue one is one of a kind!"

"Let me see that!" Ronak said and when the sales attendant first fanned it out and then draped it again on himself to show how exquisitely stunning it was, Ronak glanced at his bride-to-be, met her eyes, and without looking away, he stated, "We'll take it."

Overcome with emotion, Esha's face glowed, while the rest of the entourage looked approvingly at the couple. The sales attendant did not waste a second. Suddenly brisk, but with a self-satisfied air, he folded it quickly, and sent it right away to get the invoice made via an obvious trainee.

"What else can I show you today? Something different for the mother of the bride? Mother of the groom?" he turned his attention to the older ladies.

But now that the primary task was completed, Parul Aunty stood up to leave, explaining that she needed to leave as "there was so much to do!"

Mrs. Shroff, however, said she wanted to see a few saris to gift to immediate family members, but first called Ronak and Esha over and spoke to them in hushed tones.

"We're off to buy footwear for the big day!" Esha shared, when she returned. "Ronak's mum recommended we check “Kuhdum”. It’s a new footwear shop right around the corner.”

“Oh, right! She has to buy some heels for you, too. So fun!” Katie high-fived, remembering Parul Aunty’s explanation.

The shoe store differed slightly from the clothing store. Though the walls were paneled with mirrors, too, these showcased single sandals and shoes along the walls, and Esha almost immediately chose an open-toed sandal with gold heels and tiny blue sparkles.

“Why don’t you pick a couple more designs? Then he can bring them all out, and you can try them and compare,” Ronak suggested, and so Esha did.

They asked the sales associate if they had the three styles they liked the most in size 7, and the man said, “Yes, yes, of course!”

Then they sat down and waited. However, after a bit of back and forth between the sales agents in the backroom and the loft filled with shoe boxes, their sales attendant said, “Sorry, we don’t have the gold and blue, but we have the same style in gold and silver. May I show you that?”

"Oh, that would be perfect!" Esha replied. "If they have both silver and gold, they will get more use..."

A little while later, the man returned and apologized again. "We don't have that design at the moment. I'm sorry, but we don't have any of the three styles in size 7," he said.

"Why do you keep telling us you have something when you don't?" Ronak asked, mildly irritated.

Hearing his tone, the man at the payment counter, presumably the owner, called the sales attendant and sent him off to the backroom.

"Aaand, he's out...we won't see him again!" Esha whispered to Katie, and true to her word, they didn't see that sales attendant again. He was gone!

Another employee took over and tried to smooth things over. "Sir, tell me which ones you like, and we will order them specially...they will be here the day after tomorrow. You don't have to buy any of them if you change your mind, but we will order all the ones you like in madam's size," he assured them. "Please give me your phone number, and I will call you, myself."

"Wow...what happened to the other guy? Where do you think he was whisked off to?" asked Katie after they had stepped outside the store amidst more assurances that the shoes would definitely arrive, and he would "personally call" them.

"Not a clue," Esha replied, raising her shoulders, showing she truly didn't know. "But he annoyed a prospective customer, and so he'll be kept off the sales floor at least until we were gone, and things were smoothed over. He'll be chastised soundly at the very least," she added. "'Kuhdum' is not a big chain, and though it has two-three other locations, the store cannot afford a reputation of holding poor stock...unlike other chain stores, where it doesn't matter to any of the employees if you buy anything or not. For small businesses like these, success only comes if they provide outstanding customer service!"

"I suppose," said Katie, understanding the reasons behind receiving superlative service in almost every store, as they walked towards the car.

Sparking the Story

This story narrates my own bridal-sari-buying extravaganza to an extent. When we were shopping for my reception sari that my in-laws bought for me, my then-fiancé and now hubby and his cousin had been ushered to another room and then plied with snacks and soft drinks while we were narrowing down our options. As in the story, he, too, was invited over to help with the final decision. My mother-in-law also generously provided me with money to buy any wedding sandals I wanted, in keeping with the now-fun custom of olden days, when a bride's parents sent her off barefoot so she couldn't return home unless her in-laws gave her footwear!

The shoe-buying incident is borrowed from one of my husband's snack-shopping experiences. More eager than informed, a sales associate kept serving samples of savories that the store had run out of. After the third tasting, my husband asked, "Why do you keep offering me samples of snacks you don't have in stock? What's the point if I can't buy it?" whereupon the owner summoned the sales associate and took him off the shop floor. Another sales associate appeared immediately to salvage the sale and promised to have the items delivered the next day. Incidentally, both shops are located in the same zip code in Mumbai, and decades later, little has changed in these marketing strategies. The same courtesy is still extended to me whenever I shop at many of the exclusively upscale stores, whether I seek fineries to be worn at Indian weddings or Indian snacks.

In terms of factual accuracy, arranged marriages are still thriving, as is the custom of "who buys what" for the bride, though it varies by regions, economic ability, castes, and education levels.

5.

Somewhere in India

, the family doctor may be like family

Background information / Vocabulary:

Chawls - large tenement buildings in the crowded parts of cities and industrial centers in India for the very poor, where families inhabit tiny private living spaces and kitchens but share the gender-based lavatories and bathroom stalls on each storey

Durga-Ma - a goddess representing fierce maternal protection

Aai - the word for "Mom" or "Mother" in Marathi, one of the 22 officially-recognized languages in India

Rupees - the monetary units used in India

Buhenji or Ben - a suffix used to express deference to a lady, and translates to "Respected Sister"

Baba - a baby, usually a boy baby. However, it must be viewed in context, as it is also used to address one's father, a sage or a hermit - real or fake - and in a phrase ("Arrey, baba"), it translates to “Oh, boy!” or “Arrey, wah!” to mean “How wonderful!”

THWACK!

DR. PATEL STRUCK Ashwin on his back.

It was her fail-safe and her fastest fix to drive home the message that her instructions had to be followed, or else. She cared for him as much as she cared for all her patients, but she had neither the patience nor the inclination for any niceties. Did he think she wanted to deal at length with his foolish ifs and buts about anything at all? Did it appear she had the time to convince anyone with explanations or reasons? Had he not sat in her packed waiting room and still not realized that she could barely pause to take a deep breath between one patient and the next? No, there was nothing else she could do to make him understand at the moment but thump him.

Situated smack dab in the middle of one of the most crowded neighborhoods in the city, every seat in Dr. Patel’s clinic was taken. With the monsoon season in full swing, illnesses and infections surged all around. For her clientele comprising mill-workers, tradespeople, and other sundry blue-collar workers, Dr. Patel had been, for over twenty years, all-in-one — the pediatrician, the family-practitioner, the geriatric specialist, the allergist, the dermatologist, and like Durga-Ma, one of the many-handed goddesses, also their fierce guardian. Indeed, to her patients, she personified protective maternal care of the world because she was tireless in her efforts to cure her patients of any malady. Also, like Durga-Ma, the goddess, she was revered and feared.

It did not matter that the clinic was like an old storefront with her name, "Dr Karuna Patel," displayed on a no-nonsense, non-illuminated, black-on-white sign on it. None of her patients cared about that or that "the waiting room" was nothing fancy either — it held padded wooden benches forming two aisles, and it was open to the public once the metal shutters were rolled up. Almost like a covered porch, it did not have any glass panels or dividers, so anyone going past the clinic on foot or behind wheels in the slowly-inching traffic could easily see who was sitting there. This reception area led to an open door covered by a thick black curtain, which was the examination room, and to the left of the door, sat Savita, like a sentinel.

Savita, a self-made compounder, a.k.a. medicine dispenser and medical assistant, was Dr. Patel's "Gal Friday," her sidekick, against the ills of any season. Always neatly attired, with neither a pleat in her sari nor a strand of her curly hair out of place, she was a picture of efficiency--she made short work of any minor and messy task needed to keep the clinic running smoothly. All the patients knew this and also that she knew all about them, but they liked and respected her just as much as they admired the Doctor herself.

At the time when Dr Patel was berating Ashwin, the clinic was filled with the young, the old and the in-between, as usual.

Just like any casual passerby who could see the occupants in the waiting area, all the patients waiting there could catch any loud sounds inside the examination room, and so unfortunately for Ashwin, everyone heard and also recognized the unmistakable sound of someone being smacked. Knowing looks were exchanged, and some patients folded their lips inside their clamped mouths in futile attempts to squash their amusement but couldn't prevent a small spasm of silent laughter. Younger children, though wide-eyed, looked appropriately terrified.

"Didn't I tell you to come back and show me the medicine?" Everyone in the waiting area had their ears strained to hear Dr. Patel's scolding.

Meanwhile, Ashwin looked dazed, though the sting in his shoulder left him with no doubts about the trouble he was in. His mind was still swirling with a jumble of questions and denials.

Did she really hit him?

No, she did not.

She could NOT have hit him, could she?

No, he was thirty-one, for God's sake!

He was a husband and a father, not in sixth or seventh standard, when he had regularly driven his own Ma, his "Aai," to whoop him with her rolling pin.

No one had ever laid a hand on him or dared to even threaten him with a beating, except his beloved "Aai".

"I'm sure you're not feeling any better! Right? It's been over three weeks since you came to me with your problem," she said, glancing at the calendar on the wall. "Why didn't you come back sooner?"

"I-I didn't have enough to pay you back! And, I-I had to go to work," Ashwin blurted.

THWACK!

The second shoulder smack had come out of nowhere, and though he had arched his back in involuntary anticipation, it had shocked him out of his roiling thoughts into the distressing present.

His eyes like deer in the headlights, he was unable to utter a sound. Instinctively, his gaze flew to check on his sleeping baby, then at his wife's face, and yes, Prabha's shocked expression confirmed that, indeed, Dr. Patel had struck him.

Not once, but twice!

Why did she hit him?

Who gave her the right?

Was it because she had not only prescribed but also paid for his medicines?

No, that couldn't be it. Dr. Patel had paid for his medicines several times over the years, but she had never smacked him before!

"Did I ask you any questions about money? I asked you why you didn't come back sooner, when you were clearly not feeling better! But you–YOU–don't listen!" Dr Patel asked, through clenched teeth, still railing at him.

Ashwin's mind was still in a whirlwind. What could it be? Perhaps it was because he had not followed her instructions and returned to show her the tablets...

That had to be it!

*****

"Come back and show me the medicines," she had commanded, he remembered in a flash. He also recalled that after she had heard his complaints, she had written a prescription, opened her desk drawer, and handed him more than enough rupees to buy the medicine along with a prescription — something she was known to do. Well aware of exactly where her patients worked, exactly how much they earned, and exactly when their money ran out, which was usually a few days before payday, Dr. Patel often lent money to her patients to buy medicines.

However, slightly abashed about accepting the money, he had not wanted to trouble her anymore. And that was why, instead of returning to show her if he had the right medicine as she had commanded, he had slunk back home after filling his prescription at the pharmacy. But he had to return when he had found no relief from his symptoms.

Now, here he was, explaining himself to the doctor.

“But... but, I didn’t know!” he stammered.

“That’s right! You don’t know. Because you are such a fool, you can’t even follow simple instructions. I told you, didn’t I? Why didn’t you listen?” she countered, through clenched teeth, clearly frustrated.

She sat down, her elbow on her desk, and rested her forehead on her hand. Suspecting that he wouldn’t buy the meds if he knew they were suppositories like some patients she knew, she had thought it was best explained after he had spent the money. Swamped by patients as usual, she had failed to notice that he hadn’t returned at the time and now the fool had ingested them.

After a moment’s silence, she asked, “How on earth did you swallow those pills?”

“To be honest, the size of the pills disturbed me, so I asked Baba if I could borrow his beetle-nut cutter to chop them into smaller bits...” Ashwin said hesitantly, looking at the floor.

“Your father didn’t think to question the size of the pills either?” Dr. Patel asked, signs of mirth beginning to overtake her obvious exasperation.

”You already know my Baba very well. To tell you the truth, Baba said, ‘That’s a good doctor for you! She is not afraid to give you the strongest medicines, the biggest pills!’ You know that after all these years, he will never question your cures!” Ashwin answered.

Elbow resting on her desk, her palm still to her lined forehead, Dr Patel unexpectedly chuckled before giving in to full-blown laughter.

Ashwin stared at her, nonplussed.

Still laughing, Dr. Patel called Savita, and between chortles and outright guffaws, the two of them somehow found the words to explain to Ashwin that his medicines were suppositories, not ingestible tablets! And, much to his embarrassment, instead of questioning the size of the tablets, he had simply chopped them up and swallowed them.

Suppositories? Medicines he was supposed to...?

Hearing that, Ashwin broke out in sweat.

“Wha-what will happen to me?” he stammered, his face flushing in panic.

“Nothing. You’re still here, still alive after all these days, aren’t you?” Dr Patel replied, wiping her glasses of the tears brought on by laughing so hard, while Savita gave in to intermittent giggles though she tried to stop her petite shoulders from shaking.

“But now you need to buy some other medicines. Go get it,” Dr. Patel ordered, handing him a prescription. “And, come right back to show me. Tell them I am waiting for you. Prabha will wait right here till you come back.”

After he left, Dr. Patel instructed Prabha to sit with Savita, who was still failing to wipe the smile off her face. Prabha stood up to follow Savita out of the examination room, but stopped and turned to ask a question. A little hesitantly, she asked, “Did you ask him to get the same medicine I took the last time I had stomach issues?”

Surprised, Dr. Patel replied, “Yes! Why?”

“Buhen-ji, it had a terrible aftertaste...I am not sure that he will finish the dose,” she offered her opinion tentatively, knowing that her husband’s pre-existing aversion to bitter meds, now worsened.

Dr. Patel responded with a piercing look, and nodded.

A few minutes later, Ashwin returned with the medicine bottle for her approval, and when he came within striking distance, she did it again.

"Thwack!"

She slapped his upper arm this time. But thank heavens, she no longer looked irate. Then, she said, almost gently, "You better finish this medicine. If you don't, it will not work on you again. Hear me?"

Ashwin nodded sheepishly, like a sixth-grader who had been up to no good and had been caught red-handed.

Yes, I am a dolt, he thought, and I deserve her whacks. It's only by God's grace that I have a doctor like Dr. Patel who cares for me like a mother, just like my Aai did. Why else would she take the trouble to smack me?

Sparking the Story

Hard as it may be to believe, most family doctors I know in India do become like family. Also, a physician practicing family medicine in areas where their clientele comprises blue-collar workers, will most likely know what their patients do for a living, more or less what they earn, and often, what they eat on different days of the week.

Further, most independent practioners do not accept credit cards, and, for the most part, patients are expected to pay in cash unless they are receiving treatments at government-run facilities or clinics run by non-profit organizations. Many doctors, however, extend personal credit so that patients can work around a revolving account, and they make payments when they can. It is all done in good faith, and there are no questions asked unless patients make no payment for several months and keep showing up with minor ailments. My father-in-law and aunt-in-law both went above and beyond their calling, and extended credit to their patients without charging them any interest at all. On the other hand, there are many, many unscrupulous medical practitioners, too, like anywhere else in the world, and they prey mercilessly on the ignorance of their uneducated patients.

Also, as a rule, doctors do not smack you, but I knew one in my family who did, and I loved her very much. Her patients loved her, too, and they did not complain if she swatted them for not heeding her advice. A few have shared with me that they saw it as a caring act, an expression of her concern for them.

6

Somewhere in India

, honor hinges on how you host

Background information / Vocabulary:

Cha-cha (or Kaka) - the familial term used to address dad's brother – younger or older – often with their names as a prefix. Also, these are used to address male friends of the family

Ji - the gender-neutral suffix added to names or titles express respect

Dadu or Dada-ji - both are terms for paternal Grandfather, though "Dadu" smacks of a tone more fond than formal

Beta or Betu - beloved or dear child

Masi - the term used to address mom's sister — younger or older, derived from the words "Ma," and "si", which means "like," and so the term "Masi" means "Like Mom"

Masi-ba - the term for a grand-aunt

nimbu-paani - a homemade lemonade from freshly squeezed lime juice, sugar, salt, and water

khadi - cloth woven on a hand loom from cotton, silk, wool or from a mixture of any two or all of these yarns

henna or “mehndi” - mehndi, otherwise known as henna, is a paste of henna leaves blended with other condiments and ingredients. Most wedding traditions across India include an event a day or two before the wedding during which professional henna artists apply designs on the hands and feet of the bride and the palms of all the other womenfolk. In some parts of the country, men will also decorate their hands likewise

tola - a tola is an ancient unit of weight for precious metals, particularly gold, equivalent to 11.66 grams or 0.41 oz.

fasting-approved food - a list of foods that can be eaten during religious fasting; it usually includes all fruits, dairy, tapioca, potatoes, and “rajgira” or Kingseed / Amaranth, though the items may differ in different communities

THE DEN, WITH ITS DECOR and air of decorum, made a statement about its owner. To an astute judge of high-end elegance, it spoke volumes. The soft hum of the air-conditioner, the distinct fragrance of musk, and the polished mahogany-paneled walls decked with award plaques and framed photographs with eminent public figures and family showcased Sohanlal Sharma's standing in society, celebrated his achievements at the national and international levels, and shared some of his happiest moments with his family. From its Kashmiri silk carpet to its beautiful yet functional antique furniture and fixtures, the room breathed understated sophistication as much as it firmly expressed, "This is my world."

Seated in one of the wingback accent chairs, Roshni, the wedding planner, reined in her nervousness and attempted to make small talk about the IPL series - India's cricket matches that were always a popular topic of conversation no matter where she went these days. She had met the others in the wedding party a couple of times already — Nisha, the-bride-to-be, Nisha's parents Deepak and Chetna, and of course, Bhatt Sahib, the family business manager, as well as Heer-Chacha, a family friend who was also the trouble-shooter and fixer of sorts of all things, big and small. They were easygoing and likeable individually and also in a group, but Roshni knew well that all their plans were contingent on one person's consent — Sohanlal Sharma, the patriarch of the family, grandfather or "Dadu" of the bride-to-be Nisha, “Bapu-ji” to the rest of the household, “Sohan” to a handful of friends, but widely known as “Sharma-ji”.

Sharma-ji had the final say, Roshni had been told, and considering that this wedding would be the event of the year in this town, his decisions could mean a huge difference to her bottom line as well as her reputation as an excellent wedding-planner among the top elites. She was anxious enough to drag along Yogi, the star choreographer in her team, a rising star with his quick adaptations of any Bollywood dances to suit different age groups in any celebration. She really needed all the moral support she could get.

While they were still waiting, Chetna summoned Ramu, their full-time, live-in help.

Ramu came right away and awaited instructions.

“Chai? Coffee? Nimbu-paani?” Chetna turned towards her company and enquired, reminding Ramu to bring the different types of beverages as soon as they were made, so the tea wouldn’t be cold by the time coffee was made, and so on. When Ramu repeated the order, she added, “First bring milk for “Bapuji,” referring to a concoction with milk, turmeric, unrefined sugar, almond powder and cardamom, Sharma-ji's beverage of choice after his morning bath.

Ramu nodded, and as he left, in strode Sharma-ji, dressed in pristine white pants and a cream Khadi-silk shirt. Well into his seventies and carrying himself straight and tall, he still exuded a leonine presence, and Roshni could see why he commanded instant deference.

At the introductory meeting with the bride's parents, it had been obvious to Roshni that both Deepak and Chetna Sharma would deny their daughter little. But having never met Sharma-ji before, she was unsure about the family patriarch's reaction to the exorbitant costs of their plans. She prayed that he would approve of all their elaborate plans, but she was fully aware that there were many, many areas where slightly less expensive options could be chosen, and if the head of the family demanded any changes, she'd have to do it and somehow keep everyone happy, especially the bride. Hopefully, Sharma-ji would hand her the deposit without asking for too many modifications. The wedding was only three months away, and it was time to start paying deposits to the vendors.

Her heart hammering, Roshni handed the folder to the scion to follow along with the copy she had on her tablet. For all she knew, they could be heading right back to the drawing board.

Taking the folder from her, Sharma-ji put on his reading glasses and began reading along.

"A photo shoot with an elephant?" asked Roshni, reading aloud the first item on the list, to confirm his approval.

"Of course!" agreed Sharma-ji.

"If we're including an elephant, are we also keeping the chariot drawn by four horses to make an entrance at the reception?" asked Roshni.

"But I wanted the chariot...!" interrupted Nisha, and Chetna placed a restraining hand on her daughter's hand, silently urging acquiesce to her grandfather's wishes.

"Who says we can't have both?" asked Deepak.

Nisha beamed. "Are you sure, Papa?"

"Am I sure I want to give my princess the wedding of the year? Yes, I am sure!" said her dad.

Roshni exhaled in relief, but if someone had remarked that Chetna looked slightly more stressed, everyone else would have to agree. Chetna had no illusions about her role in this event. No matter who decided the wedding details, she'd end up having to keep an eye on it all, wedding planner or not. She was the mother of the bride and expected to have at least as many hands as Goddess Durga. She added this to her mental list of her ever-growing responsibilities for the wedding, but also decided that it was time for some damage control.

"Betu," she interrupted, addressing Nisha, "since Yogi is here, why don't you go to the drawing room and make a list of the songs you'd like to include for the dances? The sooner you decide on the soundtracks, the more practice you can schedule with your friends! Go, make a fun playlist, and leave the rest to us! Your papa and Dadu can do this much."

Indulged as thoroughly as she was, Nisha recognized the tone of her mother's voice and what that expected of her. She had best leave now.

"Oh, okay, as long as I have the chariot!" Nisha said impishly and left the room with Yogi, closing the door behind them.

"Now," said Sharma-ji, "you've heard my son, right? Remember, it needs to be the wedding of the year, the wedding of the century, ha ha! Let me see what else we have here... Fireworks? Hmm..." he nodded. He read on, his black-and-gold Montblanc pen in hand.

"Accommodation for all the guests at The ITC Heritage Hotel. Good. Conveyance to and from airports and the railway station, good, good..." and so he went, checking off the most expensive options in the list, sending Roshni in a secret tizzy. Then he looked up and directly into her eyes.

"Just one thing..." he said.

Here it comes, thought Roshni, knowing that she'd have to fulfill his requirement, no matter how unreasonable.

"I expect everything to be executed flawlessly. No holdups, no hitches and no handwringing later. It may be Nisha's wedding, but I am the host. My honor hinges on how well this function is viewed. Every aspect has to be splendid," Sharma-ji was emphatic.

Phew! Splendid, she could do, given this budget.

"Yes, absolutely. I understand," said Roshni. Exhaling in relief, she accepted the check.

*****

Over the next few months, things began coming together slowly but surely, and soon it was D-Day.

Attended by a motley crowd of about twelve-hundred guests - immediate and extended family-members from near and far as well as friends who were like family, employees of the family business along with their families - the wedding revealed Sharma-ji's generosity and affluence, and all that it could buy. No matter their station or employment position, they were all honored guests and welcomed as warmly as close kin.

Every detail had been tightened and polished and now presented in its sparkliest best. Even Kamala-Masi's dentures gleamed. The great-grand-aunt of the bride, and Sharma-ji's aunt, she needed no prompts to reprimand anyone who didn't show her due respect.

The events of the wedding celebrations flowed seamlessly, though Kamala-Masi's eyes tracked Chetna intently, her expression expressing her irate thoughts. Shouldn't Chetna have been checked to make sure I am comfortable? It is the 11th day of the lunar calendar, a day of fasting, not for any wedding revelry. Couldn't they have listened to me and moved the wedding day? No respect for elders anymore, she fumed.

Meanwhile, the henna designs on Nisha's hands and also those of the bridal party had been complimented and commented on : Most of them were shades of "Here, let me see...Beautiful! And I can spot your initials with the groom's. Oooh, I see they are inside a heart!" Of course, there were some suggestive insinuations as a few relatives loudly announced, " Look at this red-black hue? What passions have you been hiding, child? Only the fervent and fiery can end up with such a dark color!" followed by a cackling that was shredding Nisha's determined-not-to-let-anyone-ruin-my-wedding-day attitude.

The gifts had been accounted for and envied: "Those diamond earrings by her uncle are to die for! And her grandmother's pearl set...drooool!"

The jewelry worn by the bride had been assessed: "Someone said she was wearing fifty tolas of gold. Is she taking all that with her, or is it just borrowed for the day?"

The caterer was well known, and his name alone caused ripples of excitement: "Chandan-Raju Catering," said one guest to the other, compelled to say the name, and the response was a quick raise of eyebrows and a slight nod. The name warranted no comebacks, just approval.

Heer-Chacha was on top of the game, and his attention was not just on everything and everyone, he also somehow was everywhere at once. Experience had taught him that for most of the guests, good and plentiful food determined the success of the event, so he strode towards the closed kitchen doors and barged in.

Then he ran a quick eye over each of the thirty-seven dishes planned for the buffet, plus the dozen food choices for people who were "fasting." Assured that everything was under control, he walked over to chat with Gautam, the main man of the catering company.

Just then, the sous chef joined Gautam and said, "Sir, there's a problem! We have only 20 tubs of ice-cream, and we need at least forty-five! We have another sixty at the warehouse, but it will take at least an hour to fetch them in rush-hour traffic."

Heer-Chacha immediately took over. "Alright. Keep calm. Is someone at the warehouse now? Yes? Tell him to call an Uber, fill it up with the ice cream tubs, and get here as soon as he can."

Then he called three staffers, handed each a card, and instructed them to each cover specific shops in a 5-minute radius to buy all the ice-cream logs they could get their hands on – no ice-cream bars or sandwiches – get an itemized bill, and return within 15 minutes. That way, they'd prevent an embarrassing situation in case the delivery from the warehouse was stuck in traffic and didn't show up in time.

As they were leaving, he ordered, "You," pointing to the sous chef, "will serve the ice-cream we have and if you run out before we get more, you will tell the guests in line that the ice-cream cups are being washed, and ice-cream will be served as soon as that is done."

Then, he calmly walked over to Kamala-Masi with a server and said, "Kamala-Masi, come, the food is ready. Let me lead you to a table, and this young man," gesturing towards the server, "will attend to you. You do not need to wait or serve yourself in the buffet line."

"I am fasting today," Kamala-Masi said haughtily. "I doubt whether I can eat anything except ice cream."

"Oh, Kamala-Masi, how can you imagine we hadn't thought of you?" asked Heer-Chacha instantly, "You wound me. Why would you even allow such a thought? You are this family's most respected elder. We have special fare in honor of your fasts – milk halwa, and rajgriha, and tapioca..."

“What do you think? That I came here to eat?” interrupted Kamala-Masi, still refusing to be mollified, demanding the importance she felt was owed to her.

But Heer-Chacha could not be defeated – he knew the ways to win over people. Well aware that all older folk in every part of the world commonly feel invisible and irrelevant, he held out his hand to her and said, “Arrey, nah! I was given the strictest instructions by Sohan and even reminded three times by Chetna that you were to be served first before the buffet was opened to any guests, and I am just following orders. Come, come, I will serve you myself, and the server can carry your dish back to the table....” he continued cajoling her gently, and led her to the buffet table.

Sparking the Story

Indian weddings are a blitz, whether it's the sounds, the sights, the smells, or the servings of food. For one thing, the noise never stops. Neither the excited chatter nor the laughter will tone down a smidgen, not even while the priest is persevering through the ceremony with the bride, the groom, and their immediate family around the fire. Accentuating the noise is a panorama of vibrant colors. Since black is considered inauspicious and no one wants to be the harbinger of ill omens, the guests are usually clad in the fieriest of colors, as well as being bejeweled, sequined, and perfumed. Resplendent, they are ready to be stared at since staring blatantly at strangers is easily one of the nation's favorite pastimes.

The other wedding aspects that add to dazzling the senses are the aromas and the array of food servings. In a venue garlanded and lined with flowers, the smoky smells of camphor and incense blend with the wafts from heavily-laden tables of the spiced and the fried. As guests queue up to sample foods served on long buffet tables, it is easy even for a seasoned wedding-goer to forget to eat in small portions, to forget that the courses of food are unending, and to forget that there's probably another buffet of desserts that will be their undoing!

If these are not astoundingly different customs from most weddings in the West, there are a few more contrasts. There are no wedding registries, and close relatives usually tend to gift jewelry or cash to the bride. Also, friends and their guests, employees, and their families are usually invited, and unless the family has celebrity status, no one checks the invitation cards scrupulously, and no one will bat an eyelid about bringing along a visiting relative or two. In fact, it is known that college students often crash large wedding venues knowing that they can feast from a lavish wedding buffet without worrying about the tab or being turned away. And yes, though there's adequate seating, it is more common to find food offered buffet-style at weddings.

Another difference is that Indian wedding festivities last more than a day and so several outfits are required. Attendees are prepared to change their attire and their accessories at least thrice over a couple of days – for the "Sangeet" or "Mehendi" ceremony, the wedding, and then the reception, which may be held on any day of the week deemed favorable on the lunar calendar. Though every effort is made to schedule a wedding on weekends, festivities start a few days prior to the main event.

Lastly, the ice-cream incident is based on a near-miss stumble at my own wedding. Some barrels of ice-cream didn't arrive, and there was a real risk that we'd run out. However, that could have become the talk of the town, so my father-in-law's friend told everyone that the caterers were out of silverware, and once the spoons and cups were washed, the ice-cream would be served, but uh, no. He had sent some caterers out in a hurry to buy ice cream from every store near the wedding venue.

7.

Somewhere in India

, it's easier to find both sympathizers and swindlers

Background information / Vocabulary:

Rupees - the monetary units used in India

mojdis - traditional Indian footwear for men and women, also known as juttis / jootis or khussa, and typically worn during traditional events

Sa'ab - an abbreviated form of "Sahib"- a respectful way to address men, much like "Sir"

Bechara /Bechari (you) poor thing - "Bechara" is a masculine term and "Bechari" is feminine

Onion Pakodas or Pakoras - deep-fried snack bites made of sliced onions or other vegetables mixed with gram flour, spices, and herbs

Masala chai - black tea brewed with milk, sugar, and spices such as cardamom, cinnamon, ginger powder, powdered cloves, and pepper

"THREE HUNDRED RUPEES," Tejas consoled her, "eh, it could have been worse!"

Tejas was absolutely calm about it, but not Pooja. It still rankled her how the street vendor had deceived her a few days ago.

"It's not the money, it's the principle of it!" Pooja fumed, shrugging out of Tejas's sideways hug. "I hate being swindled like that!"

The incident had marred an otherwise perfect holiday for her.

She should have never gone to that outdoor bazaar again, she berated herself for the umpteenth time. Granted, she had found some great bargains – a couple of cute mementos as well as three pairs of funky earrings and a vibrant green-and-turquoise kaftan she couldn't resist. Even so, it didn't help her feel better at the moment. After all, it was her fault — she had been the one to suggest that perhaps they could stroll through the bazaar once more on their last day of vacation.

"Again? Where are you planning to wear all that fancy stuff?" Tejas had teased her.

"You needn't worry about that," she had responded, her eyebrows arched saucily, showing him her palm, "Leave that to me!"

So off they had gone again, a quick indulgence before they returned home that afternoon.

Strolling through the stalls, Tejas saw comb-like bamboo salad servers, and wondered whether to buy a pair for each of the two secretaries in the Math Department. They were constantly going way above and beyond their responsibilities, always helping out professors with a smile, even absent-minded ones like him who often needed last-minute favors.

Tejas considered himself fortunate for more reasons than wonderful coworkers. Teachers and professors were still held in high regard in his country - a "guru" or a teacher had always been considered "a dispeller of darkness" or ignorance by most people. In fact, the age-old tradition of respecting education and educators still endured despite western influence, but he did not take their deference for granted. Tejas treated his students with respect, too. He was also quick to show appreciation of his department staff – buying them edible treats to celebrate different festivals, and also when he traveled. Maybe this time, he'd buy them something different. He paused to look at the wares, and the vendor greeted him like an old friend, showing him other "new items" that would make wonderful gifts with enthusiasm. Street-savvy, he had pegged Tejas as a kind man and so, along with his sales pitch, the vendor smoothly solicitated for a donation, too.

"Sa'ab, business has just not been good enough, and I need twenty-thousand rupees to pay for my daughters' school fees...is there any way you can help?"

"Look, I am paying for the schooling of our servant's children already," Tejas said, gently but firmly, used to such requests from perfect strangers, having lived in India for most of his life. "I can empathize because I know that good schooling is expensive, but I can't help. I can't take on the responsibility of paying for a third child."

"Alright, I understand...but, please, in case you know anyone, here's my card. If you hear of anyone who is helping with educational grants, please give them my card."

The shopkeeper thrust a business card in Tejas's hand, disappointed, but unwilling to give up hope. A lifetime of consuming Bollywood movies, where sudden windfalls and generous rich humans appeared fortuitously, had immunized him against such improbabilities in real life. Tejas took the card and put it in his pocket, unwilling to quash the man's dreams of a miracle.

Meanwhile, Pooja had wandered over to the next stall, spying the most colorful slip-on shoes, mojdis, and sandals.

Struck by the vivid colors on an embroidered pair of mojdis among the many piled on a table, she checked them for the size stamped inside. Eh! It was the wrong size, but perhaps they had more inventory inside, she hoped.

She took a few steps towards the interior of the stall and then hesitated, because it was packed with buyers. Wondering if she should brave the crush of people, she paused and immediately nipped that budding idea.

No, she knew better than to go into that crowded stall. To venture into any kind of jam-packed space was to ask to be slickly robbed, or quickly groped. No, thank you, she decided and turned towards the tables outside the stall again. Perhaps she'd get lucky and, oh, wonder of wonders, she did! She spotted a mojdi with an embroidered peacock in all its glorious colors, albeit only the left shoe.

As Pooja was digging through the pile of footwear to look for the second shoe, a 10-12-year-old boy sidled up to her with several handbags hung on his shoulders and forearms.

"Auntie, will you buy a bag from me? I haven't eaten since morning...one bag is only fifty rupees. Please, Auntie, I am hungry...." he held out his wares – faux leather and canvas totes and pocketbooks.

Pooja glanced at the boy. Whitish spots marked his pinched face, and he looked gaunt and desperately hungry. Pity gnawed at her because there was not one thing right about a child of his age to look so tired and defeated. She sighed. He was probably older than she had guessed, his growth stunted by lack of nutrition. Perhaps she could buy him some food at a nearby stall even if she didn't buy his bags.

Almost immediately, one of the shop salesmen came forward attempting to chase him off. "Move on, move on ...don't trouble my customer" he snarled.

The young boy reluctantly left, and stood in the pathway between the stalls, repeating his sad marketing spiel to anyone who'd listen.

Pooja turned to the shop assistant. "Arrey, Bechara...the kid seemed hungry!"

The salesman shook his head, "Madam, don't get fooled by sad faces. You can't let these kids come too close. They often have light fingers!"

Sighing again, because he may be right and also because it would be too easy to drown in sadness by the deluge of hunger and hardship around her, Pooja quelled her sympathy and turned again towards the display of footwear. For a second, her excitement was dimmed a fraction as the inequity in her world hit her again.

Here she was, looking for yet another pair of footwear she didn't need, and there stood a child trying to scrape a living to stave off hunger, instead of being at school. It felt wrong. Sighing again, she turned away, mindful of the fact that if she allowed every pleading urchin and beggar to make her feel guilty, she'd never have a moment of joy or wonder or excitement...and life deserved all of that, too, didn't it?

Resolutely, she picked up the single mojdi and showed it to the vendor. “Do you have any more in size 7? There’s only one in here...”

“Let me check, Madam,” he replied, and off he went, undeterred by the milling customers, to the back of the stall. He rummaged a bit, then signaled a thumbs up before he held up a pair of the same mojdis held sole to sole, raising it over his head triumphantly.

“Should I wrap them up?” he called, and she gestured, “How much?” with a twist of her right hand.

“Three-hundred and fifty,” he declared, to which she countered with “Three hundred!”

The shop assistant then fake-wiped his forehead with a smile, as though to convey that she’d driven a hard bargain, but in no time, he returned, shoes wrapped in a newspaper.

Excited with her purchase at the time, she had put them in her shopping bag and joined Tejas, who had been convinced to buy a couple of bamboo trays, along with salad servers.

Pleased with themselves overall, they hurried back to the hotel, because it had begun drizzling. It was time to pack up. They began gathering their belongings strewn in their room, and stuffed their purchases, still wrapped tightly in old newspapers inside generic plastic bags given by the vendors.

They still had three hours to go, and the drizzle had turned into a downpour. While they were waiting, Pooja said, "I'm a little peck-ish. You?" bringing over the Room-Service Menu to Tejas.

They read it together, and then exclaimed in unison, "Onion pakodas!" Like many other important decisions they had usually agreed on, they were unanimous in their notion that there was no better nosh on a rainy day than onion pakodas with masala chai.

Soon, the hot tea arrived with two plates of onion pakodas. The thinly-sliced onion slices smothered in a pungently-spiced batter and fried to crispy perfection were as finger-licking good as they had expected! The aroma still lingered in the room even though their snack had been relished and long gone – the only drawback they could find in this deliciousness, besides of course, the fried part, but so worth every bite.

The rain hadn't eased yet - coming down hard, seemingly almost horizontal - and it was time for them to leave. However, their Uber ride had still not shown up, and so after they checked out of the hotel room, they figured they would wait in the reception area.

But just when they'd made themselves comfortable to read on their tablets, Tejas's phone rang.

"That's the Uber driver," Tejas shared before answering. "Hello? Yes...yes...oh...are you sure? Ok, ok, we'll come there..." Then he hung up his phone and said, "He says he's been waiting near the gate of the hotel for five minutes and there's such a queue of cars that he can't come inside. So either he could cancel the ride and then we could order another one, or he'll wait there for us...." he paused, then suggested, "But, really, there's no point in calling someone else because they, too, will face the same problem, right? Let's take our stuff and head there."

So they hoisted their backpacks and lifted their carry-on bags, not wanting to roll them in the tiny rivulets that had formed on the road. Trying to stick close together under an oversized umbrella, they fast-walked towards the gate.

Fortunately, they found their ride right away before they were completely soaked.

Meanwhile, the wind had picked up and so they hurriedly hefted their carry-on bags in the trunk. But before they could reach the door of their Uber ride, their umbrella turned inside out. With the rain lashing down, Tejas struggled to keep open the door of their Uber ride so Pooja could get in first, while a particularly strong gust seemed determined to close it. To add to the maddening mess of a monsoon day, Tejas noticed a bicyclist was riding towards them, right on the footpath!

What on earth was a cyclist doing in the rain? Was he one of those petty thieves who make off with your luggage or bumps into you for your wallet? The thoughts ran through Tejas head, so he was nonplussed by what followed.

Completely drenched as he was, the cyclist stopped right by them. Then he gripped the cab door open while Tejas struggled to tame the umbrella and shrug off his backpack before stepping inside.

"I've got the door, Uncle! I'll hold it till both of you are in!" the cyclist said, holding the door open till both of them were safely seated.

Once settled on the back seat, Tejas leaned sideways and tried to pull out his wallet to tip the cyclist, but saw the young man was wheeling away speedily. Tejas let the image soak in before he exhaled. How heartwarming it was to be helped by a perfect stranger, he thought.

As the cab inched towards the train station, Tejas realized that, in a land where it is common practice to address older people – known or unknown – as “uncle” or “auntie,” the familiarity included a privilege, too. Thanking his newly-greying hair for this kindness, he grinned. He had not only been elevated to the status of an "uncle," but had also been judged worthy of receiving unsolicited help from a young adult. Not a bad thing, this aging business.

“That was so ...nice,” Pooja remarked, for want of a better word.

With that warm finishing touch to their vacation, Tejas was now even more glad that they had taken a break from their busy schedules. Spending a few days in a small town, where people still had time for small courtesies, did a heart good.

However, the feeling of being rested and recharged after a brief break changed for Pooja as soon as she unpacked her last purchase, her lovely mojdis. When she discovered what she had been handed, she was absolutely outraged. She was raging with the “that swindler! May he get his comeuppance soon!!" and furious with herself for not checking the package he had given her. Nothing Tejas said made an iota of difference to her annoyance for having been handed two pairs of left shoes!

"For the life of me, I can't fathom why he'd do it, but it is not a mistake," Pooja insisted. When she replayed the scene in her mind to share it with Tejas, she realized that even as the shopkeeper had shown her the pair, he had held them up high but sole-to-sole to make impossible to notice his ploy.

"I should've checked!" She berated herself again and again, though Tejas patiently explained that no one typically unwraps a purchase immediately afterwards. That was exactly what the vendor was counting on and that's how she had been duped!

"Look, street vendors across the world are the same – they will try fair means or foul to make a sale, and it's all a part of bargain-hunting – you win some and you lose some. In any case, it's not worth getting so riled up about it," Tejas reiterated. "Three hundred rupees won't make us much richer or poorer."

Fortunately, Pooja agreed with his reasoning after a couple of days. She gave in, ready to let the indignance go, and let her inherent kindness take over her grievance.

"I imagine things are a little desperate in retail now that people are shopping so much online," she said. "It's easy for me to say how he should or shouldn't conduct business with all the privileges I have. Heaven knows what I'd have done to survive had I been in his shoes...no pun intended." She shrugged. She'd give the mojdis to the street cobbler down the road – he'd be able to reuse some bits and pieces to repair or renew someone's footwear.

Sparking the Story

No matter where we are in the world, it is not surprising to find unsavory behavior in a melee of humankind. In fact, the ratio of being swindled or being inappropriately touched is probably directly proportional to the sizes of a country's population. Considering that India is the most populous country in the world, we must expect the number of such incidents to rise accordingly, and it would be prudent to avoid tight or crowded spaces and check purchases before leaving any vendor stalls. Petty thievery and opportune groping is easier and so even more rampant in crowds.

Also, even though most beggars seem worthy of help, it would be an impossibly crushing task to attempt to aid each one of them because of the inordinate extent of poverty. Lastly, acts of kindness with no expectations of money or returned favors are extremely common, as are solicitations for money from perfect strangers.

India demands an incredible strength to survive, and also the ability to say "no" to both bargains and beggars.

8.

Somewhere in India

, business runs late... or on the lunar calendar

Background information / Vocabulary:

Ayurveda - an alternative, holistic medicine system with centuries-old roots in the Indian subcontinent, where it is still practiced alongside Western cures or often, independently

Amavas - a new/no moon day marked on the lunar calendar, considered inauspicious for any personal or professional dealings by many practicing Hindus

Mauli - a red and yellow thread that is often tied to the grills surrounding a shrine or a tomb of Muslim worship, and sometimes worn around their wrist after asking for a wish or a boon

IT HAD BEEN A CLOUD of misery and fear following her, Ruhi still remembered. For days, she couldn't shake off the apprehension with which she had met her mother-in-law five years ago.

"If our horoscopes don't match, that's it...she won't accept us being together," Dhir had warned her.

Even after all this time, Ruhi could easily recall how she had searched his face for humor. He was a bit of a prankster, and at first, she had only half-believed him. But, no, there wasn't the slightest hint of humor in his expression, she had noted, her heart sinking.

He had covered her hand with his and said, "Look, I'm her only child, and what if your horoscope says you'll become a young widow? She'd never agree to such a match!"

Of course, she wouldn't. No mother would. But how could Ruhi win a fight that was determined by her star alignment?

Terrified that she may be rejected for something entirely out of her control, Ruhi felt unbidden tears sliding down her cheeks. But she had turned her face away to hide them even though the thought of Dhir dying, of a life without him dug a cavernous pit in her stomach that threatened to swallow her.

"Ruhi, no." Dhir had been contrite at once, reaching out for her. "Don't cry. I'm kidding, I'm sorry! I'm so sorry! Please, please don't cry! She's not like that, I promise. I swear! And, and, look at me... will you please? I need you to believe that even if Mom disapproves of us, there's no way I could end us...I couldn't, even if I tried....I'm sorry," he had repeated, pulling her into an embrace. "I shouldn't have joked about it. I'm so sorry," he had whispered, kissing the top of her head, buried in his shoulder. Then, gently raising her chin up, he kissed her eyes, trying to stem her tears, and even when her sobs subsided to sniffles, he kept his lips pressed on her forehead.

She'd nodded then, accepting his apology, and continued nodding every time he reassured her for the next several weeks. But no matter what he said, Ruhi's anxiety was a weight pressing down on her chest, making it an effort to breathe deeply every time she thought of having to face his mom.

By the time Dhir's mom flew down to New York some months later, she was a nervous wreck. For their first meeting, her heart hammering like a drum connected to a subwoofer and getting louder with every beat, she had rung the bell to Dhir's apartment. Queasy as she waited in the corridor, she could hardly swallow.

After what seemed to be an interminable moment, though it was probably just a minute, she had heard quick footsteps nearing the door, then a slight jiggling of the doorknob before it finally surrendered, and the door opened. Divya had stood there with a smile, both her hands outstretched to clasp Ruhi's, before folding her in a longer-than-a stranger's hug.

"I am so happy. So, so happy to finally meet you!" Divya had said, and Ruhi's fears had begun crumbling in her warm embrace.

Towards the end of that visit, Ruhi had confessed how afraid she had been, and Divya had mock-glared at her son, and reassured her further. "Dhir is a rascal to have teased you so. He knows very well that we believe in a popular adage: 'If the King loves you, you're the Queen,' and Dhir loves you. He is my heart, and you are in his...and so, in mine."

Ruhi had never had any reason to doubt her words then or later, and soon addressed her as "Ma," which Divya loved.

Indeed, Divya was fiercely protective of them.

*****

Over the next three years, while Dhir and Ruhi traveled to a dozen countries across the world and while the rest of the family had clamored for news of a baby, it was Ma who always reared up like a tigress caring for her cubs again and again from any real or perceived attacks from anyone.

"Let them be...let them explore the world and each other before they are chained down by all those responsibilities!" She had told everyone to back off, even after they'd bought a house in Westchester, and even stood up to her own mother-in-law. So when Ma had called to tell them about her scheduled surgery, Ruhi's reaction did not surprise Dhir.

"I'm going," Ruhi had responded immediately. "I want to be there for her, Dhir. I can't not be there for her. She'll need us, especially after the surgery," she had reasoned, worry clouding her eyes.

With a slight frown of his own, he'd drawn her close, and murmured, "Yeah, yeah. We'll figure it out. I'll see if I can swing a few weeks of working from Mumbai."

When the enormity of her decision sunk in, she allowed herself a few minutes of panic, thinking of all that was needed to be done within the next ten days or so for three-to-four months of living in India. Where to begin winding up? There was so much to do to extricate herself from her life in the USA, even short-term.

"I can do this," she told herself after taking a deep breath, and began her list.

As a writer, she had perfected the art of shutting out the world each day to focus on the project at hand, and that's what she did — writing one task after another, and then checking them off. Of course, there was also the looming deadline for her fifth book, but she was sure she'd be able to work on it there.

Once the surgery is done, I'll be able to make a good dent into the first "shitty draft" of my book, she willed.But it was certainly an enormous relief when Dhir shared the next day, “It's settled. I'll be able to work remotely. It'll mean pulling all-nighters, but maybe I won't bother trying to get over my jet lag!”

Thank heavens Dhir was a heavy sleeper, Ruhi thought. She knew that trying to sleep during the day, even half a day, would be a challenge in India. Her experiences during her many vacations in India had taught her that in any busy household, the doorbell rang every hour or more, and to make matters worse, people seemed to like long prayers or tunes as their doorbell sounds instead of any short chimes.

Maybe she should pack her noise-cancelling headphones so she could work for a couple of hours at a stretch. After all, Ma had the household running like a well-oiled machine, with trusted servants who had been with the family for many years. Besides, it would be nice not to worry about cooking or laundry — or any household chores for that matter.

With that in mind, Ruhi looked forward to the trip, now that most of the tasks in her checklist were completed.

Besides being around for Ma, she was also excited to experience India in a more leisurely manner and the indulgences that came with full-time help, instead of the usual rushing around that had marked their vacations in their homeland. Over and above all of that, she was eager to show her gratitude for being wholly accepted right from the get-go, and to be on the giving end, for a change. Ma had always done so much for her and had never asked for anything in return. In fact, she had not asked them to come down for her surgery, and kept asking, "Are you sure it won't cause problems for you? Your work?" and Ruhi had meant it when she said, "Absolutely not! We'll figure out a way to deal with the hitches. Ma, we'd be happy to spend time with you, we'd love to come." She had meant it with all her heart.

*****

As eager as Ruhi had been to be part of Ma's care team, she now exuded annoyance at the surgeon's consulting office. Cooling their heels in the waiting room to speak with Dr. Pathak, fatigue and frustration gnawed at Ruhi' equanimity. It was hard enough to hit the ground running in India. The weather, the sheer number of people, and the non-stop noise had already been an assault on the senses. Severely jet-lagged after an eighteen-hour flight across several time zones, Ruhi felt done in.

She exhaled wearily, looking around at the bustling activity around her. Waiting Room. Aptly named, Ruhi thought. You could die waiting right here! It was good that Dhir had checked with the Dr. if it was alright not to bring Ma along since they were just stopping by for a few minutes to understand the pre-and-post care.

*****

For the nth time, she checked her watch, though the wall clock in the waiting room made it entirely unnecessary to do so — the relentlessly circling hand pointed out clearly how long they'd been waiting.

It was exactly an hour and a half past their appointment time! She was seriously ticked off.

If Ruhi wasn't so irate, she'd have seen the humor in the hands of the clock, that Dhir had noted with amusement.

"Giving time the finger..." he had murmured, laughter lurking in his words, glancing quickly at the clock to draw her attention there. When she followed his gaze, she noticed that the clock hands were shaped like a human hand with an index finger pointing at the numbers on the clock.

"Not funny!" she had hissed. "Not when I can barely keep my eyes open."

Finally, at 11:39 a.m., they were seated in Dr. Pathak's consulting room.

Dr. Pathak greeted them with a distracted smile and gestured for them to sit down on the two chairs facing him across the gleaming, glass-topped table, while he listened to someone on the phone.

This is inexcusable, Ruhi thought. He's still not ready for us.

"I see...Hmm, yes, I understand. No, no, don't worry...give the medicine a chance to work, okay? Yes, yes, we can change, but..." the Doctor was not looking at them, but turning the pages of a medical file on his desk.

Ruhi was slightly uncomfortable, wondering why the doctor was speaking with another patient in their presence. Was there no doctor-patient confidentiality?

As the doctor said, "Yes, yes, the bedsores ...I understand..." she cast a shocked expression at Dhir, who deadpanned her in return.

Trying not to focus on what was obviously another patient's condition, Ruhi let her mind wander, but soon enough realized that Dr. Pathak was talking to them. She forced herself back into the meeting. However, as he started explaining, Ruhi's mind reeled. It must be jet lag, she thought. She must have zoned out and probably had heard none of it correctly.

She shook her head slightly, as though she needed to toss her hair back. But it was really an attempt to focus, because what she had understood of the doctor's reasoning was ludicrous!

"It is in her best interest to schedule the surgery as soon as possible," Dr. Pathak was saying. "But she wanted to give you both enough time to schedule your trip and then we didn't want to schedule it on a full moon or a new moon day. I mean, we do operate on those days, but many prefer not to.... unless, of course, there's an emergency, I'd rather not," Dr. Pathak continued, rather matter of fact.

What? That seemed really bizarre!

Ruhi racked her brain for any such tales by her parents of their years in Mumbai, and not one tale regarding such traditions and nothing even remotely close came to mind.

As renowned as he was in his medical specialty, how could Dr. Pathak believe in such mumbo-jumbo?

Growing up as she had in an affluent neighborhood in Connecticut, she had heard of plenty of surgeries — both medically necessary and elective. However, these had been scheduled and completed without the least consideration of the lunar calendar! Why would doctors follow such kooky ideas and schedules? Didn't they have enough to contend with, what with having to work around the countless religious holidays they celebrated in the country?

She looked at Dhir to see his reaction. He looked unfazed, nodding as the doctor explained further, "She'll need to stay three days at the very least. You can then rent a hospital bed by the month, and we also have an agency we recommend for home healthcare."

Then Dr. Pathak pressed a buzzer, and a uniformed girl came in to collect the medical file and the two of them.

"Don't worry, your mom has no other underlying health conditions, so I don't expect any complications. The recovery period shouldn't be that long, either, okay? Please pick up your medicines at the payment counter. Asha will take you there." He gestured towards the staff member, stood up, shook Dhir's hand, and nodded to Ruhi. Then Asha ushered them out and led them to the accounts payable office?

As Dhir was paying the deposit, Ruhi noticed a small carved model of a temple hung on the wall, with three miniature idols of Ganesha in it. Someone had lit the incense stick, too, as there was an unmistakable fragrance of sandalwood in the air.

*****

Once they were in the car, Ruhi was dying to talk about the absurdity of surgery schedules having to sync with lunar calendars, but Dhir was on the phone the entire way. Once they'd reached home, he went to his "office", closed the door behind him, still on the phone.

"I don't understand. Why do they not schedule surgeries on a new moon or full moon days?" an extremely baffled Ruhi asked her mother-in-law right away. "What kind of a doctor does that?"

To her surprise, her mother-in-law was amused at her outrage. "A good doctor," she replied. "I know it may seem very strange to most people who did not grow up here…" she paused, choosing her words to explain "… BUT here, we have the advantage of blending the best of Eastern and Western medical approaches...and both the scientific and religious reasons."

"Wha-?" Ruhi squawked.

"The full moon causes high tides, doesn't it? Well, our body is about 60% water, and many of us believe that if surgeries are performed at that time, it will cause more bleeding than it would otherwise," continued her mother-in-law with a smile.

"And no moon?" Ruhi questioned, still flabbergasted.

"Oh, everyone here, including the illiterate crowd, will observe "Amavas". That's what we call the No-moon or the New-Moon Day. It's considered an inauspicious day, a 'heavy' day for humans, when people feel their most extreme selves. We all know that human emotions peak on this day because the gravitational force of the moon pulls everything upwards, and the same applies to your blood and energy," Divya explained. "In fact, you'll find that on a new moon day..."

"But what about emergencies?" Ruhi interrupted. "What if there is a horrible accident, or someone in acute distress?"

"In emergencies, we do what we must. But why make a conscious decision to bleed more if we can help it? Why choose more pain?" answered her mother-in-law, pausing to let that sink in. "Why schedule a surgery on such days?"

Then, very gently, she said, "Ruhi, there are very few parts of running a household in India that don't need a lunar calendar."

"Oh?" Ruhi's mouth shaped the word.

"Let me tell you, no vegetable vendors or handymen will show up on a new moon or a no-moon day, so you have to plan the menu accordingly, " explained her mother-in-law. "The wholesale vegetable market will also be closed on "Amavas!"

Hardly believing her ears, Ruhi still hadn't closed her mouth.

"Also, when I am bedridden, some of the help" nodding to Jankibai, who was dusting and wiping surfaces in the room "will probably go to different temples and offer a coconut or something or the other for my recovery, and if they share that with you, always offer to pay them for the expense, alright?"

Ruhi nodded uncertainly, and then asked, "But how often do I pay them? And which gods?"

Her mother-in-law smiled. "We have 33 million faces of Gods for a reason. Now, while they all represent different aspects and abilities, they are always around and available, so we can pray to any of them that our hearts tell us to..." she trailed off with a smile.

"Oh, and Mohammed will also want to buy a Mauli to pray for my quick recovery at his favorite shrine, so please offer to give him some money to buy the thread," she added, referring to the family driver, a devout Muslim.

Bemused at the depth of goodwill around them, Ruhi could only nod. Hopefully, she wouldn't mess up too much. Nothing in all her planning or her life abroad had prepared her to manage a woman's life in India, not even as privileged as she was.

Sparking the Story

According to Ayurveda, one of the oldest healing systems in the world that originated in India, the moon has a definite impact on humans — physically, mentally, and emotionally. There are many scientific journals that explain the underlying reason for this belief, how the fact that the moon influences the way tides rise and fall also affects our overall health since our bodies comprise 90% water.

In addition, it has been proved that mental health symptoms, including psychoses, appear to be more severe on these days. Even the Greek physician Hippocrates, known as the Father of Medicine, stated, "He who practices medicine without the benefit of the movement of the stars and planets is a fool.... Touch not with iron that part of the body ruled by the sign the Moon is transiting." So the linking of medicine and the moon is not confined to this country and is known since 400 BC.

These days, surgeries in India are scheduled without checking the lunar calendar, but it will not be considered irrational if a patient requests that they do. As far as people running small businesses - vegetable vendors, independent carpenters, cobblers, and others - are concerned, it may be partly a matter of self-preservation. These daily-wage earners risk financial ruin every single day, so their reasoning makes sense: why try to sell one's wares or services on a day when emotions are running amok? It is the kind of trap they cannot afford to ignore.

Lastly, people try to make deals with the divine in all cultures. Similar to the lighting of candles in churches, different religions offer many options to appease the divine. For example, some promise to offer coconuts or flower garlands to deities and/or tie sacred threads on railings of temples and mosques.

9.

Somewhere in India

, a little humaning goes a longer way

Background information / Vocabulary:

Vadodara - a city in the state of Gujarat

Coolies - licensed porters at Indian railway stations, now re-titled “sahayaks,”meaning assistants, who will carry your luggage into and out of the train, all the way to your next means of transport

coupe - a private cabin in the first-class section of the train

chevdo - a crisp, savory mix that may include variations of fried or roasted cornflakes and or puffed rice, fried savory noodles, potato sticks, raisins, nuts, and spices to taste salty, sweet, tangy, and zesty in each mouthful

Durwaan - a watchman of private residences or buildings

Baba - a baby, usually a boy baby. Also used to address one’s father, a sage or a hermit–real or fake-and in a phrase (“Arrey, baba"), it translates to "Oh, boy!" used to either commiserate or protest, so it must be interpreted in context

Ben or buhen - sister, used by itself as a noun or as a suffix after a proper name to convey respect

Bhai - brother, used by itself as a noun or as a suffix after a proper name to convey respect

Bhabhi - elder brother's wife, used by itself as a noun or as a suffix after a proper name to convey respect

compartment - a separate space within a railway carriage or coach like an open cubicle

jaan - life, often used as an endearment

Mogras - Arabian jasmine, one of the most fragrant jasmine varieties

Raat-rani - a night-blooming jasmine; literally translated, it means "Night Queen"

Sa'ab - an abbreviated form of "Sahib"- a respectful way to address men, much like "Sir"

Maharaj - a term used to address a religious guru/priest, but also as a suffix after a proper name to address a male chef or a cook in some parts of the country

naankhatai - Indian shortbread cookies made with semolina, flour, sugar, and ghee

AFTER A SHRILL WHISTLE, the train grunted and squealed in protest for being forced to slow down. Scheduled to stop at Vadodara station for exactly three minutes, it did so with apparent impatience - still hissing every ten seconds or so, while all the passengers scrambled in panic, whether they were disembarking or stepping aboard. "Hurry, hurry!" the train seemed to convey, puffing irritably. Usually, such brief stops did not worry Chirag, but this time it was different.

This time, he was not just traveling with Lila, but also with their baby boy Kyaan, and as the rocking and swaying of the train stopped, a wave of worry assailed him.

Suddenly, he feared that a three-minute halt was nowhere near enough time, so he was relieved to see the red-attired coolies waiting near the first-class compartments of the train, as they are wont to do. He had often wondered if they had a rotation system of sorts, and the thought popped up again – how did they decide who would carry the luggage of passengers traveling by Air-Conditioned First Class, First Class, or the Second Class? After all, they could charge significantly different rates depending on different tiers — passengers traveling by Second Class would rarely have the means or inclination to pay as much as those traveling in First Class-AC.

There was probably some hierarchy of sorts, he thought. Meanwhile, a couple of coolies had jumped on the steps of the train, holding on to the handlebars before the train had come to a complete standstill. Standing at the door of his coupe, Chirag nodded to the first coolie who had stepped inside the railcar. The coolie eyed the pieces of luggage and said, "Three hundred rupees. Ok, Sahib?"

"Why? Have the rates gone up?" questioned Chirag, with a slight frown. Everyone expected some haggling.

"Arrey, Sahib, we have to carry it all up and down the stairs," the coolie argued, as all porters do. "Will you need a taxi?"

"Don't be ridiculous. We're not foreigners who will fall for that outrageous amount. Two hundred, and that's it," Chirag countered. "No, no taxi. Our driver will be waiting."

"Sahib, two hundred is a rough deal, but you are my first customer of the day, so what can I say?" the porter said with a shrug. "I must accept God's will!"

Lila had been the silent spectator, watching Chirag argue without interrupting, but she raised her eyebrows in mock outrage at the porter. She was playing the negotiation game, too, along with her husband. It was important. After all, haggling was a ritual; the man would feel cheated if they agreed to the asking price right from the get-go – he'd believe he should've asked for more. But it wasn't always easy to figure out what was fair.

"If they do a good job, I will pay them their asking charge as long as it is within reason!" had always been Chirag's motto, and he paid fair rates, no questions about it, but he, too, was aware that some squabbling was the norm.

Without agreeing or arguing, the coolie tugged at the two suitcases stowed under the berth, and then hauled them out of the railway car onto the platform. Lila followed him with three-month Kyaan in her arms and then waited beside the bags to make sure no one walked off with them. Meanwhile, Chirag waited inside the train, guarding the remaining luggage - a heavy tote, a lightweight stroller, and a carry-on.

Once everything was assembled on the platform, the coolie removed the length of a red rectangular cotton cloth from his shoulders, an important accessory in his line of work, and began twisting it into a thick ring, tucking in the tasseled ends.

Placing the cloth ring on his head, he reminded them, “It’s my first earning of the day, Sahib. You can give me whatever makes you happy, and I trust you will be kind.”

Then he heaved the biggest suitcase above his head, placed it on the cloth ring, and plopped the second suitcase on top of the first one.

“Please hand me that tote and the small suitcase,” he requested, once both bags were securely atop his head. Chirag handed them, and the coolie gripped the smaller pieces of luggage in his hands, once adjusting his hold. Then Chirag took the stirring baby from Lila’s arms, slung the baby bag on his shoulder and they began their way out of the station, trailing behind the hurrying coolie.

Loaded down as he was, the coolie strode ahead, leading the way. He weaved in and out of clumps of people at a hard-to-keep-up pace, and soon they saw the line of waiting cars parked in the lane reserved for private vehicles.

“Here, Lila-ben,” they heard a voice calling, and saw Ahmed, a stocky, bald-headed, middle-aged man smile and wave at them as he opened the trunk of a small SUV.

Ahmed was the family’s driver, and his father-in-law’s number-one fan. Also, he was at the center of Chirag’s wager with Lila this time.

“That car?” The coolie asked them and headed towards it at Chirag’s nod. As Ahmed supervised the coolie, Chirag handed Kyaan to Lila and pulled out his wallet.

“Arrange it properly and it will all fit!” he heard Ahmed scold, when the coolie tossed the first bag in the trunk. While keeping an eye on the luggage placement, Ahmed hurried to open the door for Lila, who now held the baby, making sure she felt comfortably seated with the baby in her arms.

Taking out three crisp hundred-rupee notes, Chirag gave them to the coolie and said, “Go buy yourself an extra cup of tea!”

With a surprised smile and a quick bob of his head, the coolie accepted the money. Then he briefly closed his eyes and touched his forehead and his chest with the money, silently thanking his God for the first earning of the day.

Knowing that most travelers would not have paid the asking amount, Chirag's convictions went against that tide — someone who did not beg him for a handout, but relied on a back-breaking profession to make a living and worked responsibly deserved to be paid a livable rate. All in all, it was just good humaning, especially when life had been generous to him, Chirag thought to himself as he opened the door on the other side of the car and slid in.

Ahmed quickly checked to make sure that they were ready to go before starting the car and then they were on their way to his father-in-law's bungalow.

"Everybody in good health?" Ahmed asked politely, when they had inched past the crowds at the station.

"All well. How is everyone in your family doing?" Chirag asked in return, and Ahmed responded, "Everyone is doing well. My wife's knee hurts during the monsoons...but with Allah's grace, we have no other problems."

Soon they were crawling down the recognizable route to the family home, because even at 5:40 am, there were people on the streets going every which way, and it would be impossible to drive faster.

Lila, settled in the rear seat with Kyaan held against her chest, felt herself relax. Ahmed at the wheel was as comfortingly familiar as being home. Except for his increasingly peppery stubble, Ahmed did not seem to age. The crinkle of his eyes, the way he ran his hand over his bald head, and the way he drove - the sandal of his brake foot off and on the floor of the car, as usual - were all part of her life before Chirag, marriage, and baby Kyaan.

Soon they had inched their way at the closed gates of Mani Nivas, her home ever since she had learned the meaning of the word.

"Beep, beep, beeeeep!" Ahmed pressed the car horn impatiently, though it was just 6:00 a.m., a scowl replacing his usually genial expression, shaking Lila from nostalgia.

Banarasi Durwaan, the watchman, came shuffling from the side, and raised his palm in a half-salute wave as though to say, "Wait, Wait!" before he opened the iron gates.

Ahmed hmphed in impatience. Lila's eyes, sparkling with suppressed mirth, met her husband's, and she raised her eyebrows twice in quick succession. Chirag knew all about the tiered dynamics of his in-laws' household and also understood that she was reminding him of their bet.

Of course, it was all in jest. If he didn't succeed, he wouldn't lose any money, nor would it cost anything. The only thing at stake was his reputation as a negotiator with his wife, and perhaps he'd earn some good-natured ribbing at family get-togethers, if he didn't succeed.

"The deal is this," Lila had challenged, with a twinkle in her eye. "All you have to do is convince Ahmed to go to "Farsaanwala's" to get you something!"

"Farsaanwala" was their favorite hole-in-the-corner shop to buy the freshest of snacks, and they both knew that the queue of customers there was at least 30 minutes long on any given day. Sometimes, the special chevdo was gone before you reached the counter. However, winning the bet didn't hinge on being able to buy or eat the snack; it rested on convincing Ahmed to run an errand for Chirag.

*****

Now, some of their friends would have wondered how that was even a challenge. After all, wasn't Ahmed just hired help, and wasn't Chirag the son-in-law, and don't sons-in-law hold a place of honor and deference in most households? That's what most people would expect, and most of the time, they would be right, but "most" was the operative word.

They didn't know Ahmed.

Ahmed had been his father-in-law's driver for over twenty years. He considered himself his "Bhai's man," completely devoted to his boss and to all he considered to be his boss's family. No one else. He made that respectfully clear to everyone.

As far as Ahmed was concerned, sons-in-law were second-class citizens, and as he was the longest-serving man among the household staff, Ahmed refused to open the car door for any second-class citizens, let alone run an errand for them. This was one of his whims that was not only indulged, but it was also a matter of amusement in the family because of his age and his standing in the hierarchy.

On Ahmed's part, he was respectful alright to all the sons-in-law. He would even offer to delegate and supervise so that some other staff member completed any assigned task, but he, himself, was not doing anything more than that. Unless it was specifically for Bhai" or "Bhabhi," their four daughters, or any of the grandchildren, the work was below him. Sons-in-law did not warrant the honor of his services, and he would not pretend otherwise.

"Yes, yes," he'd say, "I will send Jeevan or Babu," extending the services of the other servants, "to get it done because I need to finish up...." and then present a long to-do list.

Chirag had often given Ahmed overly generous tips, and while Ahmed was unfailingly appreciative and deferential in return, he stayed formal, almost standoffish; he would help load and unload Chirag's luggage, even carry it indoors if the house servants were not around, and, God help them if they were not, but that was it. Ahmed knew exactly where his allegiance lay and whom he wanted to run around for.

This attitude didn't offend Chirag in the least. After all, rankings or pecking orders existed in every aspect of life and in all kingdoms - human, animal and even in the pantheon of gods and goddesses. Everyone had to handle hierarchies. His own status had changed drastically after Kyaan's birth, too.

As the only son of his parents, Chirag's wishes and schedules had always been a top priority in their home, until Kyaan was born. Now, everything seemed to revolve around his baby son, and here he was, escorting the little guy and Lila to her parents' home at his own parents' insistence!

"How can she manage the stroller, and the baby and the luggage on her own? Can you not see how difficult it would be?" his mom had admonished him. "You must go along to help!"

His father had been reading the newspaper. He, too, had tilted his head towards him to give him a piercing look, before dropping his eyelids down and a slight nod, indicating that he was in full agreement with the idea.

Not that he minded visiting his in-laws. He enjoyed being with his in-laws, and they adored him. It was always a fun time with the other sisters-in-law and their hubbies even though his mom-in-law was big on formalities. She treated all the sons-in-law like honored guests, but since he didn't live in town, she made sure that every meal included some of his favorite dishes.

Also, this time, he had a bet to win; he was reminded again as Ahmed pressed on the horn again, impatiently.

Whelp, the watchman was in for it, and seeing the watchman's countenance, he seemed to know it too! There was no escaping Ahmed's inevitable rebukes of any slip-shod work.

Quick to remind everyone that he was the longest-serving member, Ahmed considered himself above the rest of the household staff. He expected obedience from all the house servants at all times, and did not hesitate to rebuke any lackadaisical efforts at length. These speeches were partly scoldings and partly reminders of how others had come and gone, but he had been there for over 25 years, and he was going nowhere.

As if on cue, Chirag heard Ahmed muttering to himself. "Didn't the man know that Lila-ben was arriving today with her baby and husband? How dare he doze off between the time I drive out to the railway station and now? It was barely an hour ago! These people have to be taught the most basic bits of their duties!"

Ahmed hmphed again.

At that, Lila and Chirag exchanged a look of amusement, and then she took another deep breath of contentment. Mornings at Mani Nivas were unbeatable, the air balmy before the sun had woken up properly, and redolent with nostalgia and all her favorite sights, sounds, and smells. Inhaling the potpourri of fragrances from the trees around her parents' bungalow - the mangoes, the gooseberries, the roses, the last of the mogras, as well as the sweet scent of her baby boy's hair, she felt drunk with gratitude, almost giddy. Meanwhile, the SUV slowed to a stop right near the steps leading to a circular front porch.

Ahmed quickly stepped out of the car and moved toward the passenger-side door to open it for Lila, though it would have been easier for him to first open the door for Chirag, who was sitting directly behind the driver's seat. But Chirag knew the place of a son-in-law in Ahmed's eyes, and so, he knew better than to expect that. With an agility and speed that defied his age, Ahmed had the door opened for Lila.

Lila turned to look at her husband, attempting to smother a smile. He tapped his forearm and then flexed it in response, his eyes flashing, before she twisted back to step out of the car.

Meanwhile, Ahmed had moved right beside her and was immediately admonishing her. "Careful! Hold his head properly. Here, give Baba to me!"

Lila let him take Kyaan from her arms, knowing Ahmed would want the privilege of carrying the baby before the rest of the servants had a chance to hold him.

As he watched all of this in bemusement, Chirag was racking his brain to find a way to ask Ahmed to get that snack.

But the bet would need to be placed on hold for now, as Lila's parents rushed out to the porch in excitement, his mother-in-law taking the baby in her arms as his father-in-law hugged Lila and him.

As early as it was, the house help was up and about, including their old family cook Chaggan Maharaj, eager to see the baby.

When Lila returned from freshening up, Chaggan Maharaj asked, "Do you want to taste the rice dough?"

Lila's face lit up. She eagerly accompanied him to the kitchen and looked around. Everything around were signs that her mum had been in a right dither about their visit, wanting to indulge her son-in-law with way too many scrumptious dishes!

Now, pausing at the kitchen counter, Lila spooned a bit of the rice dough from the pressure cooker pan and tasted it. When she said nothing right away, the cook asked her, “Well? What do you say?”

“Maybe a tad more salt?” she said carefully, almost hesitantly, knowing how affronted he felt at the smallest of suggestions, and how irate his reaction would be.

She was right about feeling that twinge of apprehension. He had not changed.

“Fine! Then add it,” he snapped, sliding the clay salt jar on the kitchen counter towards her.

“How much do you think I should add? Will half a teaspoon be enough?” Lila asked him hesitantly.

“YOU tasted it. YOU said there’s less salt. So, YOU should know how much more it needs. Put it in yourself,” he answered in a huff, and so she added some salt, almost apologetically even though she had no cause to feel so. Without a word, he began to stir it in with stiff movements.

Leaving him to finish up, she hurried out of the kitchen before he asked her to taste anything else and she offended him further.

*****

Her mum had taught all of them how to hold on to wonderful help for years, and Lila leaned on her advice once again, as she knew her sisters did.

"It's not easy, but not so hard either if you can remember a few simple rules," her mum had often reminded them. "Once they've proved that they are loyal and competent, you must let them take charge of their domains for the most part...you should also let their minor whims slide. It makes them feel needed and valued. Secondly, show them you understand that they have a life of their own, too," she had advised. "A little more humaning and a little less bossing will go a long way. Way longer than any fat salary you can pay them."

*****

About 20 minutes later, they were all seated at the table, having a hot breakfast which also included stuffed vegetable puff pastries, naan-khatai, the rice dough dish called "Khichchu" Chaggan Maharaj had thrown a tantrum about, and a few other fried savories.

"Oh, don't you have the chevdo from....?" Lila asked, with an impish smile, refusing to meet Chirag's eyes.

"We do," replied her mum, understanding which brand her daughter was asking about, "but I'm afraid it's a bit stale..." she trailed off apologetically.

Aha! Inspiration struck Chirag. In her attempt to tease him, Lila had inadvertently helped him. Chirag had found the perfect ruse!

As soon as they were done with breakfast, Chirag strolled out towards the kitchen gardens and found Ahmed there.

"Ahmed?" he called.

"Yes Chirag-bhai?" Ahmed's response was immediate and respectful.

“We just finished eating breakfast, and the chevdo that Bhai likes very much is stale, so I was wondering...” Chirag trailed off.

“Oh, I can go to “Farsaanwala” now...it’s still early enough and they should still have some. If I take the scooter, it’ll take less time than the car...” offered Ahmed.

“Wait, here’s the money...please get a kilo for him, and while you’re there, would you please get me a kilo, too?” Chirag handed him a few bills. “Will that be enough?”

“Sure, of course. Two kilos in one-kilo packets, right? I will get that now!” Ahmed accepted the money, put it in his shirt pocket, and hurried to the scooter.

When Chirag heard the impatient beep, beep, at the gate, he allowed himself to smile inwardly.

Sparking the Story

Fiction or Nonfiction, stories and movies expounding the abuse of servants in India abound, and while making for moving tales of pathos, these do not present the full picture. As with everything else, there are two or more sides to that narrative.

Popular storytelling typically under-represents the strength of the unwavering loyalty and genuine affection between household help or "servants" and the families they serve. For example, many household heads pay for the education of their household-helps' children, and also other unexpected life-event expenses without charging interest. That is how the lives of staggering inequalities - the wealthy and the poor – are threaded together. Furthermore, despite the political rhetoric, Hindus and Muslims at a personal level show mutual fondness at best and mutual respect at least.

Also, there's a pecking order in the country, like everywhere else in the world. However, unlike the rest of the world, it is glaringly obvious in India because the extreme social and financial differences are easier to spot. However, the way to win over others across the layers is easy - it calls for a little give and take, a little humaning. After years of having seen my mummy, mother-in-law, sisters, and others retain loyal help for decades, it is obvious that one of its secrets is to overlook, and even indulge some of their whims and quirks.

As in other stories based on actual events and characters, this one portrays both my mother-in-law's cook and my dad's driver; they were both incorrigible in their own way, but accepted by the families they served, quirks and all. Lastly, there was no wager between hubby and me, but knowing that the driver would not run any errands for anyone other than my dad, my husband did resort to trick him with a white lie on one occasion – he told our old driver that my dad wanted chevdo from a popular local store and then tacked on his own order. Hearing that my dad wanted the snack, our driver immediately took off on his scooter to buy it. There was no other way to make him do it but to say that Dad wanted it.

Section II

Cabby Philosophy

Section Introduction

Imagine a parade where four marching bands reach a four-way intersection. There they stand, marching in place. Then everybody strides forward, but nobody gives anyone the right of way. Nobody even pauses in their playing. Weaving and worming with their horns, trumpets, and other musical instruments that have begun to sound like cacophony-makers blaring at full throttle, the participants keep going without missing a beat and barely a hair's breadth away from each other.

Now, also envision that the spectators have joined in this rumpus—crossing through and making their presence felt. Next, add some bicyclists and riders of two-wheelers -the motorcyclists and scooter-riders - all humans in a hurry, as well as the everyday pedestrians trying to reach somewhere and beggars who have nowhere to go and call the roads their home. This is not a description of any carnival—it is an extended metaphor to compare the chaotic traffic pattern on any main road in any Indian metropolitan during peak hours.

To sum up, everyone does whatever they feel like with little regard to any traffic rules. Given the thronging masses of humans and their two-wheelers, dealing with traffic jams can traumatize a first-time tourist. However, being stuck in out-of-control situations daily seems to have turned many, many cab-drivers into musing philosophers. Stoic and usually silent, they have had the time to stockpile truisms about humans and the world at large that with the slightest of encouragement, they will dispense eagerly and freely. Over the years, what my husband and I have learned from cab drivers could fill a treasure trove, though I have selected only a fistful of their wisdom for this collection.

1.

On Flying and Falling

SECONDS AFTER STEPPING on Indian soil, we slip into our old skins and begin minding everyone's business. A small clarification though—it's considered thoughtful or, at least, pretty normal to ask perfect strangers fairly personal questions. After all, only if you were an empathetic human, you'd care to hear about any stranger's life.

Here's how it went one time:

We'd had a lengthy chat with the staff manning the taxi counter at the airport, who needed to record our names and our destination address and some more details that seemed unnecessary to provide. Supposedly, this was for our protection against swindling cabbies. In any case, once we had answered all their questions, we were pumped and ready to fire our own, barely containing ourselves while our enormous suitcases were loaded and arranged in the cab.

We just about held it together till our cabby elbowed his car through the crowds spilling out from every crack, corner, and cranny of the road. But no sooner did we go past the airport checkpoint gates than we unleashed our curiosity with little ado and asked, “How’s the taxi business doing these days?”

When he said, “It is getting harder, but it’s a living...” we zapped him with more rapid-fire probes: “What led you to it? Is it a viable venture? Is it a family business?”

To our surprise, he said, “No, no, I was in the shoe business for many years!”

“Oh, really!” I interjected.

“Yes, madam. I bought and sold shoes, sandals, slippers...sold them in my small shop, even supplied to some other shops. It was good money. I was making deals left, right, and center. For six years, things kept looking up. I had it good, but unfortunately, I kept looking for this one big deal. That’s all I wanted. Just one big deal.”

“What happened?” I asked, truly interested in his story.

The cabby gave a self-deprecating laugh and admitted, "I had set my sights so high, my feet were not touching the ground anymore. But I was obsessed with the thought that if I had just one big opportunity, I could propel my entire family – my parents, my brothers, sisters, and children - elevate them all to the very top rungs of society, but it was not meant to be..."

Then he shook his head and continued, "People say life is a game of chance, but I learned that the higher you go, the bigger the fall."

"True," I agreed. "Is that what led you to change careers?"

"Yes, Madam. You see, when you fall, most people around you will disappear. It was then I found out that most people around you are not really happy when they see you fly...but fly we must. And when we fall, very few will stay around to catch us...." he paused.

"Unfortunately, yes," I agreed, interrupting his train of thought.

"... and the hardest part of falling is that your children go down with you. But as long as those you consider your own remain yours...if they still respect and love you, you have not failed completely. And though I failed in that business, I am fortunate. I have wonderful children. I tell my children, no, in fact, I have modeled a life lesson to them. They have seen from my choices that it's important to dream and also that when dreams don't come true, your story is not over..."

2.

On Tears and Blessings

WE WERE PRETENDING it was just another day, and we were only following our normal routine - watching children play cricket from the verandah, while we waited for my Uber ride. We were pretending that if we didn't utter the words "Goodbye...when will I see you again? Will I see you again?" it wouldn't be real. We were pretending, but not very well.

"Will we meet again?" she asked, a sudden panic creeping in her wobbly voice.

"Yes, Mumma, we will, I promise," I said, determined to stay calmly cheerful.

"But, but, I am ...forgetting...I am forgetting everything," whispered Mom, a tear sliding down her sunken cheeks.

"Don't, Mumma, please don't cry, please..." I was afraid that she'd get into a loop that Alzheimer's disease often subjects to its sufferers, so their mind goes round and round a single idea or emotion.

"You know what, Mumma? This time, we couldn't go for walks because you had been feeling weak. Why don't you promise me that you'll eat and exercise every day, and when you feel stronger, have Dad call me...I will come back, and we can go out together."

Mum looked at her caretaker, slightly confused, and the caretaker said, "Yes, Aunty, you start eating well and walking a little around the apartment first. Then, we'll take longer walks on the terrace, and she will come back. Every morning, we will..." The caretaker was still talking to her as I hurried down to my waiting ride.

I gave the waiting driver my address and sat back, staring out the window at the familiar landmarks.

But before I knew it, my surroundings turned hazy as tears welled and spilled, pouring out like a gushing spout. I hurriedly pulled out my handkerchief and pressed it to my mouth to muffle my sobs, but soon my shoulders caved in and shook.

"Madam, is everything okay?" the driver asked, peering at me through the rearview mirror.

I nodded, still feeling too overcome to answer.

"Should I stop to get you some cold water, Madam? Can I call someone?" he asked, showing me his phone.

Not needing to explain myself, I still felt compelled to say something, to share and so choking on my words, I was barely articulate.

"No, no. It's just, it's just so hard leaving my parents because I live so far away...especially now that they are not doing well. I don't know when I'll see my mother again and, and," I hiccupped, before adding, "if, if she will even remember me when I return." Then, to my dismay, I started crying harder, stuffing my handkerchief to my mouth.

"Yes, I understand," he said, looking at me with concern. "I understand, but no matter how far the distance, God has blessed you with such a close bond with your mother. Remember that. You are both blessed because you care for each other so much. Consider the number of instances we hear about children and parents who fight for petty reasons and then don't even look at each other, but you are not among them. Her heart will remember you and even if her mind forgets you, she will know you as her own when you meet her again..." he strove to offer me some solace.

On the entire way to my sister's home where I had been staying, he did his best to comfort me, even asking several times if I needed to stop anywhere, in case I needed something.

When we finally arrived, he reiterated as I was about to shut the door, “Don’t go with the memory of her tears, Madam, but go with God’s blessings that are held in your mother’s tears. God has blessed your mother and you because otherwise, there would not be any love or the slightest worry for each other. Don’t forget. You are both blessed!”

3.

On Cussing and Forgiving

SO ANNOYING, I thought. There's no way this guy is getting a good rating from me today.

Standing outside the building gates of our family apartment in Mumbai, I kept my eyes peeled for a white Hyundai Xcent, even as the sun burnt my forearms. There was nothing I could do about that, so I tried my best to ignore the prickling. It was too hot to scurry back to the air-conditioned comfort of the apartment, and I'd probably have to rush out again, since he was just 2 minutes away according to the app.

Five minutes later, I checked the app again and saw the car inching forward on the screen of my phone, but still nowhere in sight.

"Where is the cab?" I muttered to myself, rivulets of sweat running down my scalp and neck. At this rate, my muslin shirt will have more wet patches than not, I expected. Pulling my shirt by the first button a smidge in front of me, I blew under my chin in a futile attempt to feel less sticky.

When he finally showed up, I slipped inside the coolness of the cab the very second he braked to a stop, and breathed in relief.

After a few minutes, I asked, "Was there an accident? Is that why you are late?"

Apologetic but appearing mildly irked, he shook his head and complained, "Nooo, no, nothing like that. Just the usual traffic. So many people out all the time! Where is everybody going? And on such a hot day? There's just no relief from these crowds anywhere, anytime of the day or night in this city! It makes a man want to hide from civilization..."

I responded with noncommittal noises, still a bit irritated.

Encouraged, he ranted on, his volume going up by a few decibels. "No matter where I look, it's impossible to break through. On one side, there is a sea of people – on foot, on bicycles, scooters, motorcycles...they rush in from every direction and if any of them gets hurt, there's a crowd waiting to beat me up even if it was their fault! They'll say,

'You should've seen that poor man on the bike!' But if I'm hit by a bigger, fancier car, people will still turn against me because who has the guts to fight a rich man? The drivers of these big vehicles are the worst bullies, may they have the worst luck. They think they are as important as their bosses!"

We were moving slowly through the slow traffic, and I began to understand his frustration. So I said, "Yes, there's always sympathy for the poor and servile deference to the rich...and the rest are just crushed in the middle," but I needn't have said anything.

Revved up, he kept going full steam ahead, as though I hadn't spoken.

"Then there's this unending construction," he sputtered. " One day this road is closed, next day, the other one. No warning, no nothing. Anywhere you turn, there are dugouts and potholes and one-way streets. If that's not enough, the police are on the lookout for the most minor of offences —a cracked side-view mirror, waiting an extra minute somewhere. Just the other day, I stopped at a roadside stall for a quick cup of tea, and fortunately for me, I saw this cop walking towards my car, and I took off right away, may he die thirsting for a cup of tea!" he cursed, gearing to ramble on.

"It's hard, I know. It's hard not to wish ill on others sometimes, but it's not good karma to do that," I interrupted, softening my words with a smile.

"Yes, you are right, madam! We should forgive people for their weaknesses, their greed, their tyranny over the weak. But it's impossible to keep excusing them. Sometimes cusswords is the only drug for a moment's relief. A man cannot keep swallowing dregs of drudgery day in and day out and not swear! If I could suffer day after day and forgive day after day, too, I wouldn't be a man... I'd be, surely, I'd be God," he sputtered, still riled up. He slowed down for the red light, and then continued. "Maybe I am not accruing good karma by cussing, but at least, I am not hurting anyone... or betraying my own or my country or my, my... humanity!" he added.

I couldn't argue with that.

4.

On Dreams and Futures

AFTER PASSING one of the biggest SUVs seen on Indian roads, our cabby shook his head in disapproval. It was a cue as good as any for folk like us, who like chatting with perfect strangers, to get going.

"How is business these days?" I asked him.

"Bigger cars, bigger houses around me," he answered. "People today shorten the little time they have on this earth chasing bigger and bigger things. Going here, going there until they are going on and on without a thought..."

Shaking his head, he continued, "For a mere lifetime of seventy or eighty or even ninety years, how much do we need? They say that humans of long ago lived for at least 400 years. In those days, it made sense to build vast palaces and magnificent monuments, and generally, huge things, but now?" he shook his head again.

Looking at us in the rearview mirror, he added, "There are stories about the foolishness of mortals - stories we refuse to learn from. One story goes that during an era when humans had longer lifespans, a man lost a son who was not yet 100 years old. Heartbroken, he could barely rouse himself from his grief to eat, or bathe, or work. Then the people near and dear to him, his friends and elders, persuaded him to meet a visiting prophet.

Reluctantly, he went, and questioned the Prophet, 'Why? Why did my son die? He was so young, so good... Why?'

'Don't grieve so,' the wise man consoled him. 'Your son's death is a sign of things to come. Times are changing, and soon, this will be the norm—people will have shorter lives, and it will be a rare occurrence when a man will make it past their nineties. And also, fathers and sons will live so far apart, they will see different shades of the sky from their windows.'

Appalled, the man asked, 'If fathers and sons stop living under the same roof, will people even build homes anymore?'

‘Yes,’ replied the Prophet. ‘Men will still strive to build bigger monuments and structures and towers taller than ever before…’

‘Why?’ the man asked the Prophet, tears still rolling down his unshaven face, ‘why would anyone bother? If I were to live just for 80 or 90 years, I would just lie under the trees ...and without my sons around me, why would I bother to make anything at all?’”

This conversation being too esoteric, too removed from modern-day realities, I asked, “But what about your children’s ambitions? Your goals? Don’t you have any dreams of your own?”

Our cabby was silent, but only for a moment. Then he said softly, “What’s a dream without a future? What’s a future without your children around? It’s a journey without a shore...just a raft adrift in an ocean,” his voice trailing off.

5.

On Laughter and Learning

Background information / Vocabulary:

Wada pau – a patty made with spiced, mashed potatoes, dipped in chickpea flour and fried, then served in a small bun, which is slathered with hot chutneys (Connotative); Patty and bread

Bhai Sahib / Bhai Saab – Respected Brother (Connotative); Brother Sir (Literal)

Ji – a respectful "Yes"; A gender-neutral suffix to show respect

Arrey! – Hey + Oh; a sympathetic response to a mishap or bad news

DHIRESH AND I walked to the lone cab parked at the very end of a taxi stand. There were no other cabs in front of it, so we weren't sure if he'd be agreeable to going anywhere. The fact that he was closer, almost adjacent, to the Wada-Pau cart probably meant that he was on a break. But technically, he was still waiting in the taxi stand, so we took our chances.

The driver seemed to have just finished eating, and we could still smell the aroma of onion fritters hovering near him. When we went closer, we saw he was reading some snippets in the greasy newspaper that had held his food a minute ago, and chuckling.

"Bhai-saab, will you go to Andheri?" Dhiresh asked. That was about 20 kilometers away, or at least fifty minutes away during rush hours.

"Ji," he answered, straightening his slouch to an upright position, balling up the newspaper in his hand, and tossing it in a nearby trash bin.

We hopped into an old but immaculate cab and settled down for the ride, which would surely be longer than usual in the evening commute.

When we reached the new, much-famed flyover, Dhiresh initiated the conversation.
"This sea-link flyover certainly has made things faster to reach the suburbs," he remarked, and followed it up with a question. "Have you seen any lessening of traffic? Any difference at all?"

Our cabby snorted, but not in the least annoyed. "Ha! Not in the slightest! We have more people and more cars year after year, so no matter how many new routes or flyovers they build, we have just as many traffic jams, if not more," inching the cab forward, and continuing, "I just read that a new flyover is planned, but it will not improve matters. It cannot. You see, the real problem is that people are not changing! The population keeps growing, and no one wants to have fewer children..."

"How can we change people's ideas and behaviors? It's not a simple matter," I murmured.

"That, I am not wise enough to know!" our Cabby answered. "But here's the thing: Everyone is looking for the government to improve matters and accommodate their needs and lives, they all want SOMEBODY ELSE to help them but no one wants to help themselves ... no one seems to think that they must change to see a change around them!"

"True. How much can any government do?" Dhiresh agreed with him. "But the problem is lack of education, too..."

"Arrey, Bhai- Sahib, these days I don't know what they are teaching and what they are studying! It seems to be like the miser's gold that he counts in private, but you don't see any evidence of it anywhere else. Everybody's eyes and mind are on their phones, watching one video after another.

And if they ever look up or away from it, it's only because they are looking for help!"

The man was right, and he was not yet done sharing his thoughts and experiences.

"...I attended school through Grade 6, that's all," he claimed as though on a podium, "but I try to read anything I can get my hands on... learn from everything around me. If only people looked around, they could learn from many, many people and things around us...including dust! When I see how specks of dust can fly with the wind and how they settle in the highest places, it teaches me to keep the company of men with higher-thinking abilities, those who are looking upward, not people who are crying all the time. I see that the same dust that can fly high will only make a puddle of mud that everyone will avoid if it mixes with low-flowing water."

Dhiresh and I looked at each other. In our search for philosophical cabbies, we'd hit gold in this good man.

He peeked at us through the rearview mirror, perhaps to check if we were following along.

Assured of our continued interest, he continued, "You may not believe it, but as soon as I began to pay attention to my surroundings, I found lessons too important to ignore! I try to learn a little from everyday things, even from the car horn! I tell myself that I don't have to pay attention to every honk on the road but if many cars do so, it's quite likely that they are drawing my attention to an obvious problem, and I need to pull over and check things out. In the same way, if one or two people say some things about me...eh, I don't have to waste any time on it" he shrugged, then added, "but if many people tell me the same thing, well, I do need to stop and check myself carefully!"

"You are a good thinker," Dhiresh complimented him, "and I am sure it helps you deal with all kinds of customers..."

"Yes, but more than anything else what has helped me is remembering a saying every time I find things frustrating. It goes like this: "Learn to laugh, my brother...it is the cure-all of a hundred diseases," he said, his forefinger pointed for emphasis.

"True," I murmured, in wholehearted agreement.

After all, what can possibly be wrong about a life strategy that invites us to pay attention to our surroundings and learn to laugh in the face of frustration whenever we can?

This is home

A peaceful blend of the east and west
Heat and spice peaking to a crest
A fiery affair
Beyond compare
And this is home to me

Heaps of trash, and open drains
Filthy nooks with grimy stains
Reeky air
Beyond compare
But this is home to me

Timeless wisdom and gracious hearts
Creative arts in all its parts
A cultural fare
Beyond compare
And this is home to me

Crowds, noise, and bids for bribes
Beggars, slums, and hunger crimes
Human despair
Beyond compare
But this is home to me

Rousing myths and cricket trance
Celebrations with song and dance
Festive layers
Beyond compare
And this is home to me

Social injustice and bigotry
Public groping and misogyny
Inequity's snare
Beyond compare
But this is home to me

Nonviolence in its genes and creed
Innovations steering industrial lead
High-tech dare
Beyond compare
And this is home to me

Holy shrines and heritage sites
Small-town ways under city lights
Mountains, plateaus, sea, and sand
So much goodness in this land

It's my makeup
It's my people
It's my history
Foul or fair
India is home to me.

About the Illustrator

Poonam Hassija is a UI designer and cartoonist who believes big goals are best tackled one small (and often funny) step at a time. Her work focuses on design and finds humor and inspiration in the imperfections of life, many of which find their way into her cartoons on Instagram @sketchbook.poonam.

When she's not sketching or designing, she's managing her most creative role – being mom to two amazing boys.

About the Author

In her heart of hearts, Kirti Vyas believes she can make any art. Her head knows better, but that does not stop her from having a go at it all – crafting with paper, fabric, metal, or stone. Writing, however, has always been both her beacon and her harbor, above all.

A certified K-6, and a Secondary-School Language Arts teacher, Kirti founded Brainy Alley Classes (www.brainyalley.com) to nurture critical-thinking and teach writing to a limited number of motivated students. And she writes. She has written copy for advertisements, corporate brochures, websites, workbooks for her emerging writers, a compilation of her poems titled **Between Us, There is Verse** and is keen to explore other forms and formats. Towards that end, Kirti regularly uploads poems to her YouTube channel:

https://www.youtube.com/channel/UCk53NMgakh1c4AvErhpk8yA

A mom to two wonderful adults, Kirti lives in Connecticut with her husband and relentless supporter Dhiresh Vyas, and more than a handful of old and new friends – where the conversation often revolves around, yes, all things books!

Previous Publications by the Author:

Between Us, There is Verse is a compilation of 27 poems in a coffee-table book that includes the inspiring, the wondrous, and the heartbreaking bits of the human experience by Kirti Vyas.

With lyrical stanzas to resonate with parents and caretakers of younger children and older parents, passionate athletes, and literary savants, it also strives to resonate with many more through our unifying personal and global issues.

Stunningly presented with images shared by students, friends, and family members of the author, the book is an inspiring testament to what we can achieve together.

To purchase: https://www.brainyalley.com/bookstore

Books for Emerging Young Writers:

Not Your Average Punctuation Practice for students in middle school and high school who understand the impact of correct punctuation and want to learn, not depend on online resources/AI assistance.

S.P.A.R.K. – The retelling of five stories from the Panchatantra - the folk tales of India - each story teaching a lesson in grammar along with open-ended questions to support critical thinking for writers in Grades 4 -5.

www.ingramcontent.com/pod-product-compliance
Lightning Source LLC
LaVergne TN
LVHW050634100826
845148LV00011B/1866

* 9 7 8 1 7 3 7 5 2 0 5 3 5 *